The
Berhama
Account

By John A. Williams

The Berhama Account
Introduction to Literation (With Gilbert H. Muller)
Last Flight from Ambo Ber (Drama)
!Click Song
The Junior Bachelor Society
Mothersill and the Foxes
Captain Blackman
Flashbacks
Amistad (With Charles F. Harris)
The King God Didn't Save
The Most Native of Sons
Sons of Darkness, Sons of Light
The Man Who Cried I Am
This Is My Country Too
Sissie
Africa, Her History Lands and People
Night Song
The Angry Ones/One for New York

The
Berhama
Account

By John A. Williams

NEW HORIZON PRESS
FAR HILLS, NEW JERSEY

11/1986
amtd

Library of Congress Cataloging in Publication Data

Williams, John Alfred, 1925-
    The Berhama account.

    I. Title.
PS3573.I4495B4   1984   813'54   84-25566
ISBN 0-88282-009-5

ONE

Gary Mandarino had just finished another Dog & Pony Show for the Berhamian Cabinet, with the Prime Minister looking benevolently on. As usual, it had gone well, facts and figures rolling smoothly out of his memory, interspersed with mild warnings and gentle no-no's. Dog & Ponys always went well, though, most clients already being seduced by Mandarino's reputation as the best political public relations man in the business.

Now he was strolling back to his hotel along Dock Street which was a moving, colorful wall of tourists. Across the street, at the dock itself, the *Rotterdam* and the *Q E II* were tied up, blotting out the bay and the other side of the island. Taxis were lined up, and under the huge poinsettia trees, the drivers of horse-drawn carriages sat patiently waiting for the riders who always came.

Mandarino paused for a traffic light, wondered if any of the tourists knew what Dock Street, lined with stores and shops, really was. More than 5,000 Exempted Companies from all over the world used the street as an address, had offices there, or elsewhere on Berhama, small and large. What these businesses did or didn't do elsewhere was of no concern to Berhamian officials so long as they behaved legally on the island. Berhamians fervently believed in the free enterprise system and most of their laws were created to protect it.

All the businesses required banking systems to serve them; these, in turn, created a demand for cunning attorneys, and on Berhama this confluence created still another business that was known as "Offshore Banking." The term made Mandarino think of scuba divers stroking toward a swim-in bank. It was an extremely lucrative if secretive business and, unlike the money from tourism, none of the profits derived from it would trickle down to the average Berhamian.

Mandarino cringed at the sudden impact of metal upon metal, and as he recoiled from it, a moped with its driver still somehow attached, slithered across the road toward him. The helmeted man leaped up, literally throwing aside his vehicle, and

2

with legs and arms already scraped bloody, ran back into the street to pounce upon the car that had struck him. Inside, the driver cringed in his seat. "You bloody, fucking fool!" the mopedder screamed, yanking on the car door. Both were black Berhamians.

Out of one of the cabs now backed up in traffic emerged a huge driver. "Easy, easy, man," he said to the mopedder who, giving another mighty tug at the car door, collapsed in the street. The cab driver bent down, announced that he was all right, but obviously in shock. A pair of bobbies appeared and began directing traffic, and within minutes Mandarino heard a siren. The mopedder, stirring a bit, was whisked inside the ambulance; his vehicle was placed upon the sidewalk; a summons was written out for the driver after brief questioning and all was back to normal, the ambulance growling away.

They did not like messes, accidents, surprises in here, but when they occurred, they were quickly cleaned up.

Mandarino turned into a bright little restaurant and sat down. The accident had shaken him. He set down his case and opened the *Berhama Times*, the only daily on the island.

"Coke," he told the waitress. He folded the paper again unable to concentrate.

The problem with the Berhama account, Mandarino mused, was simple. The have-somes wanted to be have-mores and they were mainly black and ran a sometimes efficient Opposition through their Peoples Berhama Party. The PBP had grown in size and a power yet to be measured, since the riots of last year in which 25 people, half of them white, had been killed, and 300, most of them white, had been wounded. The PBP had even attracted to it some few whites.

Conversely, the Berhama United Party—the group of record that had hired Mandarino Associates—was mostly white. Its few black members, however, in the Cabinet and out, were visibly and strategically placed to enhance the idea—believed by no one on the island—that it was a truly integrated political group. In addition to the PBP threat that might materialize with the coming election, tourism was down. The riot news had hit the U.S. and Canada like a bombshell. Of all the islands in the Caribbean, Berhama had remained the most civil, the most ordered, the most secure. It was also beautiful. The black people who lived and worked on Berhama were friendly, not sullen nor sharp as so many tourists had found them to be in the Virgins, Barbados, Jamaica, the Grenadines, the Bahamas.

Stability and order had of course brought the Exempted Companies to the island. Among the world's money markets, Berhama was considered to be one of the most solid. Lebanon was finished; Mexico was pumping oil at a furious rate and no longer had to serve as a mere shelf over which money passed, and Switzerland, after all these years, was having strange problems with its younger generation. The riots put a question mark on Berhama; the new strength of the PBP was another consideration. Could Big Money work with a "Peoples' Party?"

Mandarino ordered another Coke. He half rose from his chair, thinking that he'd just seen someone he knew. Deciding that it simply could not be, he resumed his seat. He enjoyed watching the tourists. The people at the Ministry of Tourism were hopeful that visitors would start returning in record numbers this year. The tourists didn't know and didn't care about Berhama's problems—so long as they didn't ruin their vacations. They dressed for dinners, sampled one beach after another, lay in the sun, shopped and drove mopeds around the island. They thought, these tourists, that Berhama was just a pretty little island with its bobbies and red-uniformed regimental band and pastel-colored houses. They rarely saw the enclaves of the wealthy for these were not along the main roads; these sat on or near the water and nearly all had yachts tied up to private docks, and not a few had tennis courts and swimming pools. Great wealth, Mandarino had noticed, was not flashed on Berhama and those who had it found it wiser to spend it in Europe or North America than at home where, after all, there was not really a great deal to spend it on. A pop-

5

ulation of just under 60,000 did not attract the purveyors of ultra luxury items.

Sixty-thousand. Mandarino chuckled. Most of them read the rag he held in his hand for news. He studied the front page. As bad as the New York papers had become over the years—those that survived—they looked like truth burnished compared to the *Berhama Times.* The paper was owned and managed by Michael Siggonson, brother of the former Prime Minister who had been delicately booted out of office for incompetence. In Michael Siggonson the excesses of late 19th century Fleet Street and American yellow journalism flowed smoothly together. It printed news, Mandarino had concluded, the way the Los Angeles Examiner once did: a huge headline and a bullshit story of twenty lines that had little to do with the head.

There was a curious thing about the *Berhama Times,* and it was that most of the stories were written by women. The majority of the paper's staff were expatriates from the U.K. and had no permanent Berhamian status and, therefore, were subject to deportation if their working papers were not renewed every six months by their employers. Siggonson had his reporters between himself and the deep, blue sea.

But wait, just wait, Mandarino thought, until we drag all these fuckers kicking and screaming into the media age, and we turn television loose on 'em. For Mandarino had done more with and through television than Marshall MacLuhan. He had raised its rather commonplace usage to an uncommon effectiveness.

The "Dock Street Gang," the money men in the Cabinet, the men who were prominent in the Berhama United Party, the local Bilderbergs, had seen nothing yet. Sure, they needed to win the election. Well, he would win it for them.

Still, Berhama, the money men, the people, gave him a sense of uneasiness. Beneath all the drinking, the sailing, the aping of British manners and accents, they might well be as tough as that moped driver, tough and resilient and completely set in their ways.

He glanced up. He saw the woman again. Suzanne Kendrick! Quickly he peeled off a bill, grabbed his paper and attaché case and rushed outside.

"Excuse me," he said, thrusting himself through the crowd, glancing frantically up the street, " 'scuse me."

He was sure people were staring at him. No one moved fast down here except the tennis players. Now he saw her: the erect carriage, the determined, low-heeled stride. Was it so strange seeing her here? He assumed that she still lived in Westchester, on the eastern seaboard from where about half a million people traveled to Berhama each year.

Mandarino was moving closer; he could see that

her legs and arms were well-tanned. Maybe she'd been on the island for some time.

"Hi," he said, pulling up beside her and exhaling deeply. Hi, he thought to himself. Mr. Cool. Like he saw her every day on the street when, in fact, he had not seen her in six years.

He had been married then and so had she; his had ended three years ago. Mandarino wondered if her marriage was lasting. How many times had they been together? Four, five? That was all. She had turned it off.

"Hi," she answered now.

They stopped and turned to stare at each other. She smiled. "So, that was you sitting in the Lime Tree."

"You saw me?" Mandarino was now surprised.

"I *thought* I saw you. So I came back."

She looked as though she wanted to kiss him, Mandarino thought. He wanted to kiss her, but they merely stood, staring at each other, smiling. She, finally, turned to walk. He moved beside her.

"Suzanne," he said. "God, you look great, I mean—"

She laughed, touched his arm. "You look well, Gary. How's Juliet?"

He shortened his stride to match hers. "I dunno. How's Rafe?"

"You don't know?" she said quickly, turning to face him. "Are you divorced?"

"Yeah." Mandarino stopped. Suzanne stopped. "You on vacation here?"

She started to walk again. "Maybe."

Mandarino caught up with her and they matched strides again. "With Rafe?"

"No. He's an I dunno, too."

Mandarino felt a sudden small lifting of his spirit. "Divorced, too?"

"Yes."

They said nothing while walking and side-stepping tourists, until Mandarino said some moments later, "Where are you going now? *Are* you on vacation?"

"Oh, Gary," she said, and came close to him.

He put an arm around her. The tourists parted to go around them.

"What is it, babe, what?"

"It's so good to see you."

"Good to see you. You look great. Where're you staying, the Queen Hotel?"

"No. I'm using the cottage of a friend."

"Cottage," he said as they began to walk again,

9

his arm still pressed against her back. "I know these cottages. They're mansions. But let's have some lunch?"

"Okay." She had hesitated.

"There's a small hotel down here where we can have lunch right close to the bay—"

"The Trafalgar? Yes. Good." She smiled. "But what are you doing here? Not on vacation. Not with that suit and case. Whose image are you working on down here?"

They were passing the Royal Berhamian Yacht Club. Next week it would be swamped with drunken sailors who by that time would have finished the Providence—Berhama Yacht Race. The club was one of the few that had no black Berhamian members. Most of the others had tokens, at least. "Tell me first," Mandarino said, "how long have you and Rafe been divorced?"

"Two years. You?"

"Three."

"She catch you out?"

"No. But I was gone all the time. You know this business. Crazy hours, crazy people. She *thought* I was doing more than I was. Rafe catch you? No. You would have told him, then he would have left."

"Wrong. Believe it or not, you were the only one, and I didn't tell. He just left."

"He's nuts. Why, then?"

She shook her head savagely and her lips came together fast and firmly.

Mandarino dropped it. He focused for a moment on the traffic, the cars, the snarling mopeds and their helmeted drivers.

"This is not your first visit to Berhama, is it Gary?"

"No. I'm in and out. Know anything about the Berhama United Party? Been here that long?"

"Four months. The BUP? The Dock Street Gang? Prime Minister Trottingham? Christ, that's all you get in the paper. Are you working for them?"

Her voice had risen on "them" and she had stopped again. Mandarino pressed softly against her back. "C'mon. Tell you all about it over lunch."

"They won't lose the election. Even if we were not involved they wouldn't lose it. It'd be close and they might lose some seats, but they'd win." Mandarino felt at peace now, with Suzanne sitting across from him. They were waiting for the second drink. Across the bay they could see the pink, beige, white and blue houses, flecks of colors resting on the low hillside. "Now that we're here, though, they'll win bigger. It's the next election they really have to worry about, but they don't seem to be terribly concerned. We probably won't be asked back for that one because we will have done so well on this one."

11

"So it's pretty much all in the bag."

Mandarino stared at the water. "It looks that way. Sometimes it feels that way. But something's going on. The black people here aren't all that happy. Our people are edgy. I mean, they look at the kids here who're all into this Reggae shit, and wearing African national colors. Black power salutes and handshakes. Even some of the white kids. But they're basically apolitical. They don't have much else to do here except to race their bikes and be into something. It's their older brothers and sisters, even some of their parents, and PBP keeps working them."

"Yes, but I understand that most people, black and white, take all the PBP rhetoric with a grain of salt. I should say a large dose. It's the BUP they don't trust."

"Why not?"

Suzanne shrugged. "They've been there before. In the U.S. In South Africa. In Rhodesia, England, Canada. Some news does manage to get here, and Berhamians are the world's greatest travelers. They know. Besides, they've lived with the Dock Street Gang for centuries."

The second round of drinks came followed closely by the food.

"It's nice here," Suzanne said. "Funny. I hardly ever think of coming here. So peaceful and not at all crowded." She nodded her head toward another couple seated across the garden from them.

The 12:30 ferry to Canterbury Hook was steaming out, causing several smaller vessels to rock in its wake. Mandarino could see the superstructures of the great liners from where he sat.

"So," he said. "How's it feel to be running a modeling agency instead of working for one?"

"It's all right. I was putting on so much weight, you know, that I couldn't—and then I decided to, you know, go into business."

Mandarino looked at her very carefully. A bit heavier, but that was all. Her breasts were always large for a model, but she did well in sweater and blouse things, the three-quarter shots. And the face: as fantastic as ever. Better. All of her, though, every millimeter. "Just like always," he said. "Perfect."

"No. Not anymore."

"Perfect. Perfect. Perfect."

"No," she smiled, "but, how long are you here for?"

"Just until day after tomorrow. I'll be back late next week, though. I'd take you to dinner tonight, but I gotta do it with the Prime Minister. Lunch tomorrow?"

She heard the urgency in his voice and smiled

13

with remembering, but it made her lower her head. She picked at her salad. "Sure," she said. "Shall I meet you at the Queen? You are staying there? That's where everyone stays."

"Will you? Hey. How long are you going to be down here?"

She seemed to gaze past him to the 30-footer outward bound with *Lucky Lady* painted on its stern. "Oh, I don't know. I don't know. I just wanted to get away without making plans, without having my life tied down to time, to appointments, to people." She was still picking at her salad.

"Mandarino reached across the table and took off her sunglasses. "I want to look at you," he said. "You don't sound so—" He saw the sadness, as visible as blight, clotted in her eyes, and also what he thought, fleetingly, was shame.

"Hey, babes," he said softly, putting down his fork and taking her hands. "Don't be sad. I didn't mean to walk any place I wasn't supposed to."

"You didn't." She replaced her glasses.

"Well, look, I don't—anything I can do? I mean, I can cancel the dinner tonight."

Suzanne leaned across the table and kissed him. "Sweet Gary. No. I'm all right. Honest. I just have these private things—"

"What, is the agency in trouble? I can help. Or

14

I'll get you in politics. Ella Grasso and Bella Abzug and Shirley Chisholm can make it, with your looks you could be president."

"No."

"Some jerk of a guy?"

"No!"

Mandarino sat back tense and puzzled. She seemed to gather herself. "I'm all right," she said, and stroked his hand.

"Can I call you tonight after I've finished with the Prime Cut?"

"For talk?" she asked quickly, and then, more slowly, "Sure. Of course." She wrote her number on a napkin and stood. "I've got to go now. Talk to you tonight."

"It'll be okay?" Mandarino asked.

"Yes, Gary. I'm sorry. Forgive me."

"Nothing to forgive. "It's nothing." She started up the walk to the street. "Hey," Mandarino whispered loudly. She stopped. "I still like you a lot."

Suzanne smiled and nodded and went through the gate.

Mandarino finished his coffee, paid the bill and walked slowly to the Queen Hotel. He'd call New York, take a swim, go over some notes and have a nap.

TWO

In the A suite on the top floor of the Queen Hotel,
Fern Cromwell sprawled on the chaise of the balcony. It overlooked the swimming pool and the
bay. Good to be back, she thought. Good to be
back. She picked up the gin and tonic from the
floor beside her and drank the entire contents,
brushing aside the lime with her tongue. It would
help to put her out. The G&T together with the
drinks she'd gotten in first class, yes, wow, they
would help to put her out. And she needed the
rest, she told herself. Getting away and boozing it
up and getting some good loving. Oh, yes. Away
from cameras and cameramen and sound men and

16

editors. Away from the bullshit, the news, the importance of delivering it, of being *on camera.*

She spread her legs and let the sea breeze stroke her upper thighs. Yes, she thought again. Yes. Solid strokes for solid folks. Cromwell snapped a look at her watch. Two hours before he came on duty. She'd left the message. She was still intrigued by the operator's proprietary tone:

"Mr. Archibald? Oh, Miss, Mr. Archibald is not at the bell desk anymore. He's at the *front* desk and not due on until four. Can I help you with anything else? Can I refer you to anyone else?"

Cromwell pumped her leg remembering. "Just ask him to please call 1020 for Ms. Cromwell. Got that? Cromwell, 1020."

"Yes, yes." *Click.*

But Cromwell had two hours to wait. Maybe, she thought, a quick swim would help get me out, and she rose with the thought, went inside and pulled her swim suit from the drawer where she'd placed her clothes not quite an hour ago.

Dressed in her suit, she stood before the mirror. Okay, she thought. Some puckering in the thighs, some slight gatherings at the elbows, but what the hell else could you expect at 42? Besides, those puckers and gathers ain't what you do it with. She slipped on her oversized sunglasses and plopped a large-brimmed hat on her head, then grimaced at herself. She pulled on her hip-length red terry-cloth robe and left the suite.

As she strode past the Settler's Bar in the lobby, she reflected that she might as well pick up another tall one to take with her to drink after she'd done two or three laps. She went to the bar to order, passing a man in wet trunks who looked vaguely familiar. She did not, however, stop or turn. Some renegade Congressman, she thought. Out of the corner of her eye she saw him take a seat, bend over his drink, which had a straw.

A rum drink, she thought and then she knew who it was. Shit. Is that Gary Mandarino? What's he doing here? Is there a story in it? Mandarino never takes vacations, so there must be something going on here. What? What could it be? The elections? What is so important about Berhamian elections? Those riots? But, he costs big bucks. Must be important.

Even as she ordered and paid for her drink, Fern Cromwell felt agitated, indefinably angry. She walked rapidly to the pool without looking backward; she was thinking of what she knew of the network's affiliate down here. Small station. Seven people on staff, not including the techs. They used 3/4-inch tape, got delayed broadcasts out of New York—24-hour delay—except for some events that went out via satellite. But hell, she could tape in the morning and have it run to New York for direct feed or to Atlanta via Delta or Boston via Eastern,

Delta or American for an indirect. She felt better
with a delivery system worked out. All she needed
now, she thought as she selected a chaise at the far
end of the pool, set down her drink, pulled off her
hat and glasses and curled her toes over the pool's
edge ready to dive, was the story. Cromwell
checked herself, backed away from the pool and
took off her robe. *Dummo!* she whispered to herself
and dove into the pool.

As soon as Mandarino turned on the television
set for the news he recalled who the woman was.
He smiled to himself and sipped his rum. He knot-
ted his tie and slipped on his jacket. Lightweight
suits flattered him, he thought. Made him look less
flashy, less like a gone-to-fat athlete. He finished
his drink and went to stand on the balcony for a
moment. Tonight, he knew, would be the time for
the Prime Minister's private Dog & Pony Show. He
snapped his fingers softly. Anthony Eden, an Anthony Eden type, but with more sense, more humanity, more of an eye on the future. How could
he have missed it? Mandarino went back inside and
switched to the other channel. Mudd was substi-
tuting for Cronkite. Good. Cronkite laid down the
law, like God; Mudd asked if there was any law
around. Mandarino turned the switch again. Wal-
ters and Reasoner. Burns and Allen? Fibber McGee
and Molly? Rhett and Scarlet? He turned off the
set. Of course it was all show biz. Just wait till he
brought the greatest show on earth to Berhama!

He glanced around the room and left, plunging

into the hot and humid hallway. He made quickly for the elevator, wiped his forehead while waiting for it. When it came, he hesitated a moment before stepping into the mass of dinner dresses, dark dress suits and white-on-white shirts. Inside, though, the perfumes of the women made him think of Suzanne Kendrick. When he called, would she invite him over? Would she come to him? Would they *be* together at all?

He thought of warm nights like this in New York when he had met her at Stu's at the end of the day. Stu owed him, so Stu had set up his studio like a small apartment those nights when Mandarino met her.

Stu knew the touches; wine, flowers and, of course, the lighting. Mandarino remembered in the elevator and thought of Suzanne's perfumes, of Suzanne.

But why was she so sad, he wondered as he left the elevator and walked slowly across the lobby past The Settlers' Bar. Mandarino also noticed the serene but all-encompassing glances of the door-men, bellmen, bartenders, waiters.

Maybe, he thought, she'll tell me what's bothering her. He had stopped before a poster-photo of Jax Bendersen, the rock star. Bendersen would be in Berhama playing during the celebrations for the yacht race. And getting lotsa bucks, Mandarino thought. Well. He did not understand rock music;

he was of another time—Sinatra, Como, Bennett who'd changed his Italian name, Damone, LaRosa. Christ, even Caruso was better than these rock guys.

In the parking lot in front of the hotel, Mandarino saw the polished blue Humber with the flags attached at the same time a man approached him from the side. "Mr. Mandarino?"

Mandarino turned. "Hi. You from the Prime Minister?"

"Yes, sir." The man had a ready smile. "The car's over there."

They walked to it. The driver opened a rear door and Mandarino got in.

As they eased out of the driveway, Mandarino saw a man in a tuxedo driving up to the hotel on a moped. On a previous visit he had seen a woman riding one, her evening dress pulled up to her thighs. He liked the idea of formality riding a moped. The film people could use that contrast. It was what made Berhama distinctive.

After ten minutes on the main road, the driver turned off onto a bumpy, rock-strewn dirt road that was posted with no less than 10 (or perhaps 15) different names and arrows. Slowly now, as dusk gathered beyond the low hill, the driver turned and accelerated.

Mandarino had the impression that he was moving from the front lines back, back to headquarters. The homes they passed on the darkening curves shaded with trees were not pastel-colored; they were boldly white, uniformly so, with green shutters, and they were ramblingly huge. Finally, they crested and dipped again, curved again and the driver slowed and curved once more around a grove of mangrove trees, and suddenly cruised into a paved parking lot.

"Here we are, Sir." The driver seemed to move very quickly from his seat to the rear door. Mandarino got out, glimpsing a tennis court between the trees. Nice, he thought, very nice. He found a walk that led down to the house, and stiffened suddenly when a uniformed police officer, young and pale and with a Guard's moustache, ran lightly up the stairs past him. The policemen wore Bermuda shorts in the summer, just like all Berhamians, black and white, who considered themselves to be members of the establishment. Bermuda shorts, Bermuda socks. They were the uniform of a class.

But Mandarino was cursing himself. Why had he tensed? That Mafia bullshit had gotten to him. He was sure that whenever he took on a new account, the client did extensive checking to see if he was "connected" or not. And there were always the jokes, the innuendoes, the customs people who, seeing that the last name ended in a vowel, asked questions, made him open his bag, spoke his name loudly so others would know.

22

He had never gotten used to it, never would. Mandarino wondered where Trottingham had gone to check him out. Certainly he would not be here without that.

Mandarino continued down the stairs, the hard heels of his shoes rapping against their surfaces. Now he could see the cove beyond the rooftop of the house, and the yacht, its white fibreglass hull reflecting the setting sun, riding gently at anchor, pitching easily with the tide. All tucked away, Mandarino thought. It's all tucked away.

"Mr. Mandarino?"

The voice came as he was taking the second level, down and around the front of the house. Mandarino stopped and turned. She had been watching me, he thought.

As big as she was, she seemed to be gliding toward him, her hand outstretched, in one long glance studying him from his shoes to the way his hair was combed. She was dressed in a tight, full-length gown. Mandarino knew that she was German. She reminded him in a way of some German women who were in Brecht's circle. She was ample and vaguely attractive.

"You remember me," she said. "I'm Greta."

"Yes, of course," Mandarino said. He extended both hands.

"Good of you to come," she said. She folded her

hands on her stomach. "And have you been all right since we saw you last?"

The proper hostess, Mandarino thought. "Yes, I'm all right. We're starting to crank up for the primaries, but it isn't too bad yet. How've you been? Kirkland looks tired. He ought to take a vacation." Trottingham avoided taking vacations because he didn't think any of his ministers, especially the Deputy Prime Minister, could handle the job if he went away. Didn't trust his own system.

"Oh, but we're healthy enough," she said. "Come along, won't you? Kirkland's just finishing up with his dressing. He plays for at least an hour when he comes home." She had inclined her head toward the tennis court. "And vacation? A couple of days here and there."

Mandarino followed her around the front of the house, watching her large haunches shifting and bouncing against the confines of her dress. Greta was like a Reubens come to life, perhaps a little smaller.

"None of the white guys, and many of the black guys," Brooks had told him, "marry from the island. They marry Europeans, Americans, Canadians, Jamaicans, Barbadians and the like. I guess they're afraid of too much inbreeding. They've been together on that fuckin' island four hundred years. They all have relatives coming out of the woodwork. And the relatives, just like in the American South, are black and white."

24

Brooks was the firm's resource man.

Mandarino and Greta Trottingham passed through the foyer of the house whose walls were filled with steel engravings of Dürer and Blake, and through rooms quietly elegant with cedar and rosewood walls, period furniture, porcelain vases and bowls.

"Is your room at the hotel all right?" They had stopped in a room where the furniture looked more comfortable. A large window opened on the bay and gave a view of the yacht, the islets that dotted the bay, and the other side of the island. A bar stood beside the window.

"The room is all right," Mandarino said. "This is some place you have here, Mrs. Trottingham. It's just fantastic."

Mrs. Trottingham smiled, slightly thick lips pulling back over large teeth. "Thank you. What can I give you to drink?"

Mandarino quickly looked over the bar. "Rum? Do you have any rum?"

He saw Mrs. Trottingham, with the fake expression poor actresses use, look over the bar. "Oh, dear, Mr. Mandarino. We don't seem to have any rum at all."

Mandarino grunted softly. "Well, then, scotch will do."

"Over ice? With water? Neat?"

"Neat," Mandarino said. "About four fingers."

She raised her brows and poured.

"That's fine. Thanks."

Greta Trottingham picked up her own drink and led the way to an oversized couch and a table filled with cheeses and crackers. She gestured toward the plates. "Let me help you."

"No, no," Mandarino said quickly. "Not just yet. Tell me, do you play tennis, too?"

"Oh, yes," she said. "And you?"

"I just hit the ball," he said. "I'm not very good." He wondered if Trottingham was any good.

"Oh, it's like a religion with us." She laughed softly. "And on weekends, we're always on the water. As a matter of fact, we're having Wahoo steaks for dinner. Kirkland caught one last week. It's a delicious fish. You do like fish, Mr. Mandarino?"

"Love it."

Greta Trottingham waved her arm toward the walls and the photographs upon them. "Our children. All away at school. They hated fish!"

Brooks also had reported that everyone who could afford to, black and white, sent their children away to school—to Europe, Canada or the States.

"Where do they go?" Mandarino asked.

26

"Allen's at Cambridge, Walther's at Oxford and Dinah's at Smith. Do you yourself have children?"

Mandarino smiling, said, "No. I'm not even married anymore." Brooks had also said that the whites have as many kids as they can, hoping to catch up with the black population. Their educations must cost a bundle, Mandarino thought. But then Trottingham had a bundle.

"Oh, I am sorry," Greta Trottingham said.

Mandarino shrugged. "It has its advantages." He leaned forward. "Mrs. Trottingham, would you have any objections to our working you into the campaign? You know, little kids, the elderly, hospitals, photos, appearances with the Prime Minister, public service radio and television messages?"

"Not at all. Anything I can do to help Kirkland."

"Good! I think you'll be a big help." Mandarino looked at his empty glass. "Can I help myself?"

"Please do."

"Please do what?" Kirkland Trottingham said, bouncing into the room wearing maroon Bermuda shorts, maroon knee socks and a white shirt. He was a short man and had a full head of curly hair and bulging, suspicious eyes. He grasped Mandarino's hand. "Hallo, Gary. So good to see you. Here, let me have that. Neat was it?" He glanced at the glass.

"Yes, neat."

27

"He wanted rum, Dear, but we don't have any. We must order some tomorrow."

Trottingham stood motionless for a moment, as if receiving some message. "Oh! Yes, of course, Greta." He poured Mandarino's scotch, then mixed himself a hefty gin and tonic.

"That was a great presentation you did this morning," Trottingham said when they were seated. "It satisfied everyone." He flashed his quick smile.

"I thought it went well," Mandarino agreed. "Even DeSilva and Donnelly liked it."

DeSilva was one of the two Portuguese in the Cabinet. Donnelly, one of the four black men. Both sat in the front benches. DeSilva was Minister without portfolio, charged with overseeing the Ministry of Information. Donnelly was Minister of Home Affairs. They were, together with others in both the front and back benches, hostile to Trottingham.

Trottingham snorted. "Yes, for the time being. But I don't trust them—as well as several others—as far as I could throw this house."

The Prime Minister spoke quickly, his voice in the upper registers. He crossed a short, fat leg and rested it unsteadily upon the other thigh and continued talking about the members of his Cabinet. Mandarino listened, smiled, interrupted and had another drink. Some of the stories about the ministers he had heard before, several times, but he

28

had never met a politician who didn't take the time to badly run down some of the people he was closely associated with.

The last of the daylight had eased out upon the sea, suffusing the horizon with orange, velvet-like light. The lights from the houses on the islets and from the homes on the hillside across the bay pecked weakly at the night. Greta Trottingham got up to see how the dinner was coming.

"We want to stress even more than we have already," Mandarino said, "your personal commitment as well as Government's commitment to total integration. We've got to keep pounding that into the ground, Kirkland."

Trottingham hunched his shoulders. "But of course. We *are* committed. By all means, do."

"Your wife says she'll be glad to help in the campaigning. She'll be good, Kirkland; a big help. Lends stability and assurance."

"Yes, she's very good, and she likes the people, you know. Likes them very much."

Unless they drink rum, Mandarino thought. Maybe the Trottinghams feel that rum-drinkers are low people.

Trottingham said, "Have you any idea when your film people will start? That's what everyone's waiting for, you know," he said with a chuckle. "They think you're going to make them all film stars."

"We will take the key people in your government, the Parliamentarians who're in for tough battles, and do spots for them. And you. Then you and them together, to lend continuity and a team concept."

Mandarino shifted so that he faced Trottingham more directly.

I'd like to model you after Anthony Eden. Before that Suez business brought him down. You have some combat medals from World War II, and you were Minister without portfolio to the United Nations when it began—" Mandarino flagged his hands. "—do it without mentioning Eden, of course, and you have the looks. . . ."

Trottingham ran a hand through his hair. He recrossed his leg; he alternately smiled and looked serious. "Of, course, if *having* an image is important—"

"That's the name of this game, Kirkland," Mandarino said. "You and your wife have certain God-given attributes and you might as well use them."

"Anthony Eden," Trottingham murmured. "Anthony Eden."

Jesus Christ, he's blushing, Mandarino thought.

"Come, gentlemen," Greta said, leaning into the room. "Dinner is ready. Come along."

"Well," said Trottingham, beaming at the head

30

of the immaculately set table. "We should get a break from Siggonson's paper this week because of the yacht race."

"Oh, I dread that," Greta Trottingham said. "We will have to entertain and everyone will be thirstier than usual after four days on the water." She was sitting at the foot of the table. Mandarino sat at one side. More porcelain, he thought. But this was Meissen, not Dutch.

"I see the stores all cranked up," Mandarino said.

"This year's the biggest," Trottingham said. "One hundred and seventy boats. And this year the IOR and the MSH divisions are split so that both the hot boats and the old boats can compete. A man spends a fortune for a yacht and in a few years, by most racing standards, they're obsolete because of fibreglass. We've made it possible for the older boats to stay in competition."

"IOR is International Offshore," Greta Trottingham said. "And MSH is Measurement Handicap."

"Yes, yes," Trottingham said. "The hot ship this year is supposed to be a 57-foot sloop owned by a Jewish fellow from up there. When we open the divisions it's hard to, you know, maintain the old standards."

Trottingham's wife seemed to shoot a glance at her husband. She leaned forward, her breasts

31

pressing partly against the table and said, "For example, there's a man 65 years old with a very old boat who's wanted to be in the race for years. The new divisions made that possible, but a 65-year-old man fighting all that sail and wind? I only hope to God that his crew isn't composed of senior citizens, too."

"Bloody good, Grettie," Trottingham said, throwing back his head and laughing. "Good, good. Yes, that's what happens when you change the standards."

"Maybe I'll be back for the finish," Mandarino said. "That should be something. If so, Levy'll be with me, and maybe Brooks."

"Of course. Good men, both. And know their work," Trottingham said.

Mandarino laughed to himself. Trottingham no doubt was still trying to figure out how an Italian without Mafia connections, a Jew and a Black managed to get together and make something work. He laughed to himself all the way back to the hotel.

"Hey, Sooz. Did I wake you?" Mandarino was calling from the lobby of the hotel, just in case she might want him to come over.

"Ohhh, Gary. Yes, I'm afraid you did, but that's all right.

Mandarino had a feeling. "How about a drink, Sooz? Your place or mine?"

She sighed. "Gary, can I please have a raincheck? I'm sorry, but I'm just not up to it tonight."

"Tomorrow?" he asked.

"Let's make it the next time you're back. All right?"

"Whatever you say, babes."

When Mandarino got on the elevator, he nodded to the young black man he had seen come from behind the desk and follow him down the hall to the car.

"Evening, Sir," Sinclair Archibald said, and then, "Good night," when Mandarino got off on his floor. Archibald pressed the button again for the tenth floor.

THREE

Sinclair Archibald felt a combination of emotions as he left the elevator. Sadness, fear, anger. She would expect him to be as he had been almost two years ago. Young, eager, a bloody satyr capable of bouncing around on a bed from midnight until dawn.

Things were different now. He had married the Miss Berhama of two years ago, and he had been promoted rather rapidly, too. He had, of course, purchased a house at an outrageous price that was now standard, and he had a son. In Berhama it was important to keep the nose clean, keep up appearances for, on an island the size of Berhama, someone was always watching and waiting for you to make a mistake.

True, Fern had given him the money to finish his hotel college courses at Paul Smith's; he was indeed indebted to her. But he thought he had paid the debt in full. Transactions were always made in the hotel; unattractive women, older women, younger, attractive women, all looking for pleasure without question, often tipping extremely well for that pleasuring, accepting the transient relationships without question. They were the norm. He hoped Fern would not be unlike the others. Archibald hoped so, but he sensed that Fern, having given him the money, believed his sexual obligations to her were without limit. He wondered if all black American women were like that.

"Ah," Cromwell said, pushing open the door and wrapping her arms around his neck. "Here is my Jim Brown, Sidney Poitier, Harry Belafonte and Terry Carter rolled into one. Come on in here and let me look at you."

Archibald, smiling, closed the door behind him. He liked her perfume. And he liked what she was wearing but, he thought, it's late and I want to get home.

"Oh, Sinclair, how marvelous to see you again. You've put on some weight, my darling."

Archibald patted his stomach. "A little. You look as always, gorgeous, Fern."

35

"No kiss?" she said suspiciously.

Archibald kissed her. Her tongue insisted itself on his lips. He opened his mouth. Her tongue shot inside like a thing gone crazy. She sucked his tongue until the roots hurt. When he was able, he said,

"Hey, Fern—" But she was at him again and his will was melting fast. Behind her head he looked at his watch, calculated his time, created small fictions to explain his lateness to his wife. He pulled rein on his will, but lust was ballooning in his pants.

"I've got to go," Archibald said.

"Oh, no." For a moment her strength frightened him.

"Really, Fern," he said, still wondering how he could possibly stay.

"What do you mean, you've got to go?" she said snappishly.

He made her sit on the bed. They were breathing heavily. "I'm married now. I have a family, a son. A good life. I'm not interested in all this anymore. I just want to be friends."

Cromwell lay back on the bed and, hoisting her gown said,

"Eat my pussy."

Archibald laughed, but it was not a hearty laugh.

36

"C'mon," she whispered, pulling at her clothes. She lay nude on the bed, her arms stretched up to him. "Just do it, Sinclair."

He bent and stroked her face. Her arms went around his neck and she pulled her body close to his. "All right," he said. "All right." He melted down to her.

When finally he raised himself, she pulled him back. This was not what she had planned. She had looked forward to being with him, going to the beaches, the out-of-the-way clubs, the private little parties that never broke up until the morning tide came in. Through all the pawings by congressmen, the fights with film editors and news directors, through all the lonely hours when she arrived at her apartment on A Street, too tired, too disgusted to do anything but drink, she'd looked forward to these few days to unwind. And now, what was he saying? That he had to go home? To a wife and child? She struck at him with her fingernails, driving him off the bed and across the floor.

"Hey!" he said, surprised.

"Bastard!" she screamed at him.

He doesn't know who you are, the gin whispered. He doesn't appreciate you, the gin whispered. His wife must be young and firm and good-looking, the gin whispered—*he's* good-looking. She flew at him, arms flailing, breasts twirling and bouncing. He caught her by the wrists.

God! Archibald thought. She's drunk, she's *hot!* "Listen, Fern, listen—"

Cromwell arched back her head and opened her mouth in a scream. It started low in her body and raced upward. "rrRRRAAPPEE! RAPE!"

Archibald clamped a hand over her mouth. "No, Fern, no!" She kicked at him. In his fear he felt himself growing weaker. She bit his hand. Who was this old woman to blunder into his life like this, to demand more than the rules ever called for? She was crazy. If she kept screaming, he'd be out of a job in an hour. On Berhama, news travelling the way it did, no other hotel would take him; he would be the one who got caught. Cynthia and David, what would happen to them?

As he held her, he tried to listen above their heavy breathing to sounds that might be coming down the hall. He heard none. There were not as many rooms up here in the suite section. Archibald whispered, "Fern, come on, calm down. Can't we talk? Can't we talk?"

She twisted suddenly from his hand, took a deep breath, but as she started to scream once again Archibald, in desperation, lashed out with a punch that caught her on the point of the jaw. Cromwell spun around and went down on her knees.

"Fern," Archibald pleaded, going to her.

"You fucker," she hissed, and took another deep breath.

Archibald hit her again, driving her through the door onto the balcony.

Frightened now, Cromwell scrambled to get away from him. She rose unsteadily, fighting to keep from vomiting, twisting first one way and then another and then slipped without a sound over the railing.

Archibald stood motionless, waiting for the sound that would punctuate a segment of his life. He heard nothing, and shaking, he quickly pulled his clothing together and left the room.

The morning shift workers at the Queen Hotel arrived on foot, by moped and by car. They came one by one in the blissfully cooling morning, the wind whipping playfully through the gardens that surrounded the hotel. In another hour the sun would be coming up and it would become hot and humid. But for now it was pleasant.

A laundry worker, sauntering to his station at the rear of the hotel just off the pool, thought he heard some of his co-workers talking. He hurried around the corner to join the conversation; he was, after all, ten minutes early.

He hurried now, past the six-foot, 200-year-old privet hedge that bordered the garden. "This is Fern Cromwell, NBC News, Washington. This is Fern Cromwell, NBC News, Washington."

The laundry worker had already passed the hedge. He stopped and cautiously returned to it, noticing how badly splayed and ragged it was. He peered to its top and his eyes met those of a naked black—actually brown—woman's. "Eat my pussy," she said.

The Laundry worker, a man of about sixty who had seen just about everything going on at the Queen in his twenty-five year's service there, felt a sudden compulsion to shift his weight from one foot to the other. He peered quickly around, and then raising himself to the tips of his toes whispered, "Now?"

Peter Frithe whistled tunelessly as he went carefully about his work. The old Berhama stone structure in which he moved was tucked among the ancient volcanic folds of St. Gregory's. It had been built in 1901 by Boer War prisoners who had been shipped to the island; it was for the solitary confinement of the most rebellious of Jan Smuts' soldiers.

From the single window, which had been cut into the house after the war, Frithe could see the Ramada Inn high on a distant cliff. The promontory overlooked St. Gregory's channel through which all ships had to pass to get to Wellington. The competitors in the Provincetown–Berhama race would be sighted first from the balconies of the Ramada.

These first sightings would signal the coming together of most of the representatives of great
wealth in the western hemisphere. There would be
scions and sons of scions, bankers and sons of
bankers, multinational heads, old money and new.
It came together every year in Berhama, the money,
and invariably those who owned it dressed in im-
maculate white pants and elegantly tailored blue
blazers.

Rattery had spelled it all out for Frithe, even
though Frithe had known it all his life, being a
Berhamian. But this year, Frithe thought, it would
be different.

Finished with the hand grenades, he placed them
carefully in a knapsack. They felt heavy, danger-
ous. He buckled the sack and put it away in a corner
and covered it with some soft and rank cardboard
which, when he picked it up, uncovered a fleet of
flying roaches. He waved them away.

He took a broom and began to sweep the floor
clear of sand. All was in readiness; all awaited the
arrival of big, red-haired Graham Rattery.

"Peter!" Frithe whirled at the sound and pro-
pelled himself to the window. He thought he recognized the voice; he wondered at the mix of
urgency and fear he heard in it. He saw Sinclair
Archibald—still in his green jacket and black pants
Queen Hotel management uniform—burst through
the foliage of hibiscus and oleander. Frithe, before

moving to open the door, waited to see if anyone else was coming, chasing Archibald. Seeing no one, he unbolted the door and pulled it back at the precise moment Archibald arrived at it.

"Sin! What the—" Frithe slammed and bolted the door and looked out the window again. "What the hell's going on?" Frithe was frightened.

Archibald stood in the middle of the room, his chest heaving, sweat popping from his face. "Ah Peter, I've gone and done it! Pussy's been my downfall."

"Hey, hey!" Frithe twisted from Archibald to the window. "What're you talking about? Shaking? Why are you running? What's happened?" Trembling, Frithe handed Archibald a can of warm beer. God, Frithe thought. Not now. Not *now*!

And yet he felt the allegiance of years. They had grown up together, gone away to Saranac Lake to hotel school together. While Archibald had struggled through the system in the traditional way, Frithe, after a year or two in various hotels, had become a union organizer, the first one on the island. Once not so long ago, he held the life and death of Berhama in his hands. He had only to threaten to call a general strike of his hotel workers, and they got raises. The alternative, as everyone knew, would have been the breakdown of the economy.

Sinclair Archibald had benefited from the raises

and the demands for more promotion for black Berhamians. Then came the crunch: more demands for money, promotions and time off, for pension and health benefits. Or, a series of general strikes. The Dock Street Gang had said no—an answer that had jarred Frithe until he understood that they had theirs and the people who would suffer the most would be the hotel workers and their families. For the workers had their homes or were buying them, had their cars or were buying them, their clothes and vacations. Life was good and it was in the present, not the future. His workers split, then splintered, and fell into fragments and the union now was all but powerless. No hotel would even hire Frithe now; he was a troublemaker. Unemployment was his punishment, his disgrace. He often reflected that he was fortunate not to have had a family. His only real friendship was with the man now cringing before him. Not now, Frithe thought again. Not now when, finally, I can get enough of a bundle of money to get away from this island. And that thought saddened him, for he loved Berhama, which is to say, that he loved what it might have become, what he had thought it would become when he and Archibald were young.

"Now, man," he said gently, watching Archibald gulp down the beer. "You wouldn't be the first man done in by pussy."

"It was that damned Fern. Fern."

"Ah yes, is she back? What happened?"

Archibald burst into tears, "Peter, I have killed her dead!"

God, no! Frithe thought. He grabbed Archibald by the shoulders, glancing behind him at the window as he did. "What do you mean, boy?"

"She summoned me—you know how she is—she summoned me to her rooms. She didn't know that I got married, had a child—man, it's been two years!"

"Yes, yes!"

"She kept pulling on me, pulling on me—"

"Yes, then, then—"

"I went ahead and did it. But she—"

"What *happened*, Sin?"

"I punched her."

"Yes."

"Off the balcony."

Frithe now backed up. "Off the fifth floor? Where she stays?"

Archibald nodded, watched closely for his friend's reaction.

"Gawtdamn!" Frithe shouted. "Gawtdamn, Sin!"

"I didn't mean to do it."

"She's *dead*?" Frithe went to the window again.

44

"I couldn't think of any place else to go," Archibald said. "Yes, she's got to be dead."

"They'll hang you," Frithe said matter-of-factly. "You know how they are when it comes to the tourists. We have to be nice to them; they're our bread and butter. When did this happen, Sin?"

"Last night."

"Been home?"

"No."

"What're you gonna do?"

"I don't know."

"They know it's you?"

Archibald raised his head suddenly. "I don't know. She did leave a message for me."

It took a long time for Frithe to answer. "You've got me on the spot, you know, Sin. They'd like nothing better than to catch me in something like this. Accessory after the fact or something."

Archibald went to him. "I wasn't thinking. I'm sorry."

"You're sure she's dead?" Frithe asked in a monotone, knowing that bodies did not bounce from the fifth floor of a building.

Archibald shrugged. "How can you live after a fall like that?"

"We used to have so much fun in here," Frithe said, remembering the hikes they took from Wellington to camp there, and remembering the girls they brought there when they were older. "And now," he said. "It's all turned to shit." He faced Archibald squarely. "And now what?"

Archibald shrugged then looked at Frithe pleadingly. "Can you tell Cynthia? Something, anything, but not, you know—"

"Hell, Sin. What can I tell her? You should have done that last night."

They remained in silence. The heat of the sun now seemed to be working its way through the thick walls of the house. They heard the long, flat groan of a plane taking off from the airport. The sound increased, became for moments the center of all things as the plane passed overhead, climbing in a slow turn to the northwest. The sound faded to a querulous rumble.

Frithe wished himself upon the plane. He glanced at his watch. The Eastern flight to Philadelphia. A stop in New York.

And Archibald thought of the flight, but he thought more about last night and wished he could begin time all over again and somehow either eliminate last night or Fern Cromwell. "Peter," he said at last. "What're you doing here, anyway?"

Frithe turned to answer him. The plane gave a

final rumble that passed through the skies like the weak ending of a series of spasms. "Why, dear old friend, I am in the process of saving Berhama, insuring her longevity—"

"What kind of nonsense are you talking, Peter?"

"I just told you, Sin. Now, let's see what we're to do with you."

FOUR

"Oh, goddamn," Kirkland Trottingham said. He said it like "got ham," as though he did not wish to be too blasphemous. He reached for the private phone. He no longer knew to how many people he'd given the number and then asked them not to use it except in emergency.

But then everyone had an emergency. This minister or that; that officer of the party or this one; this or that member of what Trottingham called, instead of the Dock Street Gang, "The Group." Even goddamn newspaper people, he thought. "Hello." "Yes, he's gone. Decided to take the morning Eastern flight back. What? Oh, yes, we had him out to dinner last night. One of those things in this business, you know."

Trottingham looked at his watch. "There is that, yes. But, it's unavoidable. He comes from New York and I don't bloody well see how he can not have, as it were, too much of New York in him."

Trottingham's secretary eased into the room and gave him a note. She was 25 and had the hazel eyes so many Berhamians had, together with a tantalizingly *café au lait* color. She walked from the room as though fully conscious of his eyes on her backside. "Well," Trottingham said, stroking his curly hair. "He wants us to push hard on this integration theme, so we can pick up more black voters, of course. Yes, yes. Judiciously, of course. Oh! While I have you—let me ask you this and then I've got to go. We're looking for someone black to take a directorship in the bank." Trottingham meant *his* bank. "I want all the feedback on people I can get. Insurance. We want the right kind of fellow, you know. Fair education, active on the island, stable family relationships, no playing around, at least no obvious playing around and with the right women. Do let me know."

Trottingham hung up and pressed a buzzer. His driver, now in a brown suit, entered and closed the door quietly. "Morning, Sir."

Trottingham smiled. He gestured to the couch and leaned back in his chair. "What have you, Outerbridge?"

49

Outerbridge had played cricket and tennis in his younger days. They still called him, when he sometimes sauntered through the clubs, "Old Superbat." He was a large man whose soft voice detracted from his size. As Trottingham waited, he wondered if anyone ever knew what was really on Outerbridge's mind. Perhaps not even the Special Branch chief, under whom Outerbridge worked directly on the PM's detail.

"I returned him directly to the hotel. He didn't leave it." Outerbridge then consulted his pad. "He called a Suzanne Kendrick, an American on holiday here, but they didn't get together." Outerbridge smiled thinly. "Maybe that's why he left this morning. Kendrick's been here four months. She was a model in New York. Divorced, like Mandarino, no children."

Trottingham wondered why Greta disliked Outerbridge. He was unobtrusive. He knew his place. And he was efficient and trustworthy. "That's it?" he asked.

"On Mandarino. We almost had a bad one, though, at the Queen." Outerbridge smiled again as Trottingham hunched forward. The man loved gossip and he was pretty good at gossiping himself. "You do remember Fern Cromwell, the American woman newscaster?" Outerbridge watched as Trottingham tried to recall the name. Blandly Outerbridge said, "She used to come down two or three times a year and then she made the big time and hasn't been down so often. She's down now, first time in two years. She had wanted to do an interview with you," Outerbridge said patiently. Then said, "Black woman."

Trottingham's eyes snapped open. "Oh," he said slowly. "Yes, I recall now." Trottingham fought hard not to blush. Outerbridge knew why he hadn't granted the interview. She was black, therefore, powerless. Had it been Chancellor or Brinkley—any white correspondent—he knew he would have done it. And so did Outerbridge.

"She got pretty hot last night," Outerbridge said. "Nearly falling down hot. In fact, she did fall. Young Sinclair Archibald was with her." Outerbridge let the point sink in. "You remember him. He's an assistant manager now at the Queen. Anyway, the Cromwell woman fell off her balcony—"

Trottingham came halfway out of his seat.

"—but she fell on top of those old privet hedges. She was scratched up pretty good, but otherwise is okay." Outerbridge paused. "She's also got a couple of black eyes. Archibald gave them to her, it appears."

"Does anyone know?"

"A couple of people."

"Bloody Christ!" Trottingham said. "By this afternoon it'll be all over the island. Hummm. Archibald, you say? Isn't he married?"

51

Outerbridge laughed softly. "Aren't we all, Sir?"

Trottingham feigned laughter, too. "Heh, heh, heh. Is she pressing charges?"

"No, Sir."

"Where's Archibald, still at the hotel?"

"He doesn't go until four, but he seems to have run away, thinking that the Cromwell woman was badly hurt."

"Serves him right," Trottingham said petulantly.

"He'll turn up. The matter's not at all serious."

Trottingham exhaled. "Anything else?"

"No, sir."

"Okay thanks, Outerbridge."

Outerbridge stood and gave Trottingham a soft salute and left the office.

The buzzer rang and Trottingham snatched it up. Amanda, his secretary, said, "It's Linda Churchill from the *Times*, Mr. Trottingham. She wants to talk to you. Says she heard the New York public relations man was in town."

"Tell her that I don't have any comment on that, Amanda." He hung up, thinking, That bloody reporter's going to drive me crazy. And once again he was forced to wonder who in the Cabinet was keeping Siggonson and his reporters aware of Mandarino and his people's movements while in Berhama. Secrets, confidences, bloody fuck! Trottingham thought. In almost any other country public relations was an acceptable political tool. In Berhama the use of Mandarino Associates lent an air of desperation to the fortunes of the BUP.

Ida Jones-Williams was already talking about the BUP's expenditure for public relations services. "We must be close to winning!" She would end every speech, "And we will win!" Williams was the PBP leader, a huge, gimlet-eyed woman with considerable range in her voice. She owned a small hotel on the east shore, and had been compared to Fanny Lou Hamer of Mississippi.

Of course, if Siggonson and his reporters ever discovered just how much Dock Street was paying Mandarino, that would make some news.

Trottingham was still thinking about it when his twelve noon appointment showed up. Douglas MacKenzie *was* Dock Street. His family line ran straight back to the arrival at the island of the prison ship, *Stag. Stag*, which had weathered, but not well, a storm, put into St. Gregory's, unable to proceed to Ft. Ogelthorpe, Georgia. That first MacKenzie's fellow convicts died before their sentences were finished; he survived. A free man, he had no trade, and so he formed a small group which, getting word that a sail had been sighted on the horizon undertook to go out to the reefs in small boats and set torches.

Naturally, the men aboard the ships believed the torches to be guiding lights through the treacherous Berhama reefs. In fact, MacKenzie's Crews, as they were called, did not lead the ships through the reefs, but upon them. The first MacKenzie fortune came from plundering ships wrecked upon the reefs.

But times changed and the MacKenzies changed with them. After some pirateering with Blackbeard and Bonnet, some African slave-trading, some salt-farming, the MacKenzies started two stores, one in Wellington and the other in St. Gregory's. This was in addition to land speculation and profiteering during the American Civil War.

Trottingham both admired and despised this old Scot's family that represented millions upon millions in old money and just as much in the new. Trottingham's was all new money, made since the end of World War I, when his grandfather bought up all the army canteens the British government would sell him for two shillings each. They were sold at 15 shillings each, and the Trottinghams were on the way. But there was the deference to old money as to royalty.

Trottingham led MacKenzie, in his 70s, to the couch. After Douglas the line continued. There would always be a MacKenzie, Trottingham thought. There was one now sailing down from Providence on a 40-foot sloop; another in Parliament. The Trottinghams had thought it wise to team up with the

MacKenzies. Therefore, in several different businesses the names Trottingham and MacKenzie, Ltd. or MacKenzie and Trottingham, Ltd. were painted on the doors or hung over them. All "The Group" did that—interwove their businesses among themselves, leaving few loopholes for outsiders. At times their businesses did not mix with their politics.

"Well, Douglas," Trottingham said, forcing a cheerful quality to his voice. "What brings you into town today?"

"Just talk, Kirkland," he snapped. "You know, they wanted me to take this damned job at least five times, Kirkland, at least five and I turned it down. Now I wish I hadn't."

White hair, white mustaches, a red face that never tanned but just got redder, and a drinker's nose, pitted and large. Trottingham tried not to stare too hard. "You would have made a good Prime Minister, Douglas. The very best."

"Don't sweet talk me, Kirkland. How is all this foolishness going over with those people from New York? Jasper tells me that that Italian fellow spoke to the Cabinet yesterday. When's he gonna stop talking and do what must be done?"

"All must be placed in order, Douglas. These fellows have their methods and they've proved to be very successful. We checked their records very carefully, as you bloody well know, and they are terrific."

MacKenzie snorted. "Didn't need them in the first place. All you had to do was what we have to do. You just can't keep skipping around the fact that the black people here—who still outnumber us two to one, Kirkland—have to have a bigger piece of our pie. Bloody fuckin' nonsense to pay these people all that money when we could be giving it to our own folk one way or the other."

Trottingham nodded and bent his head. That's what they all told him; the blacks had to have a bigger slice. Intellectually, Trottingham understood that and agreed with it. Emotionally, however, he wished he could get some accord from "The Group" that he, Kirkland Trottingham, was in charge here and that they should not panic. He did not feel, indeed he had never felt, that after 400 years they had to bend to the blacks. A little, of course, here and there. But "The Group" could carry on, talking up the old belief in the free enterprise system and what's more, still make a good profit without caving in to the fear that if the blacks won the next election it would all be gone. That fear was why Trottingham imagined MacKenzie was there now; they were willing to have left just a piece of the action in order to maintain a semblance of the whole. The Prime Minister believed they could keep the whole thing.

"Douglas, you really don't mean that you want us to go the way of the Bahamas, do you? That's a real mess. The radicals chased all the qualified people away, and they've been in a recession ever since. If it were not for the gambling, they'd have gone down the drain a long time ago."

MacKenzie peered out from beneath his furry eyebrows. "We seem to be talking about two different things, Kirkland. You're talking about money, and I'm simply talking about what is right."

"Heh, heh," Trottingham laughed nervously. MacKenzie talking about what is right? He knew that MacKenzie, along with several others in "The Group," had been paying some delinquent bills of the PBP, had been making available some monies for certain entertainments for its officers. Bloody hell! And why was he looking for a black to assign as director of his bank? The same reason. Insurance. Just in case something *did* happen. Just in case Mandarino's polls were wrong. Just in case. . . . And then they could all go to the PBP and Ida Jones-Williams and say: Look here, now. Don't nationalize our businesses. We helped you out. See. Here are the receipts. We're on your side. We can help you run the country, help entice the Exempt Companies to stay.

Trottingham said, "Douglas, I'm going to tell you something. I don't give a bloody fuck whether you tell anyone else or not. But sometimes I wake up soaking with sweat. I wonder if we're doing it right or if we're doing anything at all."

"That's all well and good," MacKenzie said, "but

look here, Kirkland, you can't keep running about establishing new ministries like Community Affairs, which should be so important, with a budget of only $55,000, $40,000 of which is for salaries, wages and rent on the building. I saw that budget. If Ida Jones-Williams saw it, she would have you by the big beans, Kirkland. And another thing: I read that speech of yours suggesting voluntary wage controls." MacKenzie gestured expansively. "Do you think these people are fools, Kirkland? I don't know what's wrong with you young people—"

"I'm 52 years old," Trottingham snapped.

"Sometimes you behave more like 22," MacKenzie said, unperturbed. "But what I was *going* to say, Kirkland, is that you're so obvious. How in the world can you suggest voluntary wage controls without in the same breath suggesting price controls? You've set the haves against the have-nots, can't you see? You've said that you, your administration, *us*, Dock Street, are for our making money while we curtail their ability to earn it."

"No, no, no," Trottingham said. "The paper misquoted me."

"Humph! That's what you've said ever since you've been in office, Kirkland. They are always misquoting you."

Trottingham looked at his watch.

"Lunch time, I suppose," MacKenzie said, pushing up from the couch.

"Oh, is it?" Trottingham said, springing to his feet and glancing once again at his watch.

MacKenzie looked at him and shook his head sadly. "Frankly," he said, "I sometimes wonder if we didn't make a grave mistake, booting Basil Siggonson out and taking you in. Because of his brother Michael's paper, as you know, he's gaining support."

Trottingham stood with his mouth opened. But when he saw that MacKenzie had seen his expression, he closed it and made the muscles in his jaws move up and down.

"In all fairness, Kirkland, I have to warn you that there is some agreement among "The Group" that you've got to put more sail into this project, and quickly!"

MacKenzie walked out, his footsteps sounding angry even on the gray-carpeted floor. Trottingham thumbed his nose at his back and rushed to clear up his desk for lunch.

When Roi Donnelly called to say that the New York PR man was in town, Linda Churchill had grasped the information the way a drowning swimmer reaches for straw. But Donnelly was not the only minister who had called. In fact about half the backbench and half the frontbench had tried to reach her, each minister trying to court her favor.

Churchill was grateful, no doubt about that, but the ministers didn't really expect that she would fuck each and every one of them each time they called, did they? Lord. But Michael Siggonson had called her in to make her aware that her expatriate residency was up for review in another two weeks, and that he really didn't know what to do, since her work hadn't been of the quality he thought it should be. The warning was clear. Churchill didn't want to return to England; there was nothing for her there. At least in Berhama it was warm and the taxes were minimal, and she could get to the U.S. from time to time, and quite cheaply, too. Her work was cut out for her, clearly.

Ordinarily, she did not call the ministers until well into the afternoon, but this was a different situation. She had called the Prime Minister at his office. No comment, indeed, she had thought, rushing out of the office to go to the Cabinet Building. Churchill looked like 18 with her long light brown hair, small oval face and slight figure. She was, she knew, good-looking, but it was the tits that got them. She had not worn a bra; she needed everything going for her.

Now she waited beside the Prime Minister's car, toying with the flags and glancing down at her nipples, which she could see through her gauze blouse. She saw old MacKenzie stomp out of the building, and quickly rubbed her nipples with her forearms; she felt them hardening, thrusting against the cloth.

Kirkland Trottingham, rushing out of the building to his car, which he drove himself at lunch time, did not recognize Churchill. Usually she was in jeans and shirt, her hair uncombed and without make-up. Now she was in a short skirt, combed, made-up and—

"Mr. Trottingham," Churchill said. Once she was sensitive about her cockney accent, but decided as she traveled from England to Germany, Italy and Spain before arriving on Berhama, that most people didn't know or care about the difference between a cockney and an upperclass accent; both were British. "I am sorry to bother you, but about this Mandarino from New York, Sir—"

Trottingham caught himself gazing through the blouse. "I don't have anything to say about that, er ah, which one are you?"

"Churchill, Sir. Linda Churchill."

"Ah, yes, Miss Churchill. You'll have news in due course." Trottingham opened his car door.

Churchill leaned forward. "He spoke to the Cabinet yesterday I'm told, Sir. Can you tell me what he said?"

"I have no comment on any of this, Miss Churchill."

"Was it about government business or BUP business, Sir?" She leaned into the window; one of her breasts, of its own accord it seemed, tumbled out of her blouse. "Oops," she said. She pushed it back in and held her pencil poised over her pad.

Annoyed,—strangely, not *terribly* annoyed—Trottingham said, "Well, you know he can't be involved in the government's business. We take advice from no one. Government is government."

"Does that mean, Sir, that he's here on party business? If so, then what was he doing addressing the Cabinet?"

Trottingham slammed his opened hand against the outside of the car door. "I do not wish to discuss it," and drove off as Churchill jumped back.

She began to write: Suggest head reading, "I DO NOT WISH TO DISCUSS IT!" She slammed shut her pad and said in the direction of the car, "Bloody asshole."

She walked to the other side of the Cabinet Building and unchained her helmet from the handlebar of her moped and put it on. They're so bloody snide, she thought. They're Oswald Moselys playing, and badly, John Kennedys. Cruising through Victoria Street, she wondered how she could get her hands on the poll that Mandarino's people had taken over the phones. The doo-doo had really hit the fan when they were running that. Mandarino had brought Berhama and its people kicking and screaming into the tail-end of the Twentieth Century. It would be marvelous to work for an outfit like that; leave all this petty, though vicious, nonsense behind. In the meantime, if she could get her hands on that poll she could save her job.

FIVE

Peter Frithe had read the paper and seen nothing about a dead Fern Cromwell. The radio news had not reported a dead Fern Cromwell, and there had been no bulletins over television, he knew, because he would have been told about them.

Arriving in Wellington, since he was on his way to see that Graham Rattery's quarters were all settled, Frithe decided to sound out the Queen Hotel grapevine.

Standing astride his moped, he had a quick, low conversation with a mixed black-Portuguese gardener, who then called a hotel boy who carried the message deep inside the bowels of the hotel: *Is Fern Cromwell in 520 all right?*

The boy, an unknowledgeable Rasta, put the question to his favorite cook, the one who least treated him like the Idiot of Wellington, and he, a rotund, short man, strangely civil for a cook, politely passed it on to the Chef; and he, always conscious that *he* was the center of the Queen Hotel universe insofar as he saw to the culinary needs of the 1,550 guests and another 1,500 diners from other hotels on the island, sent for the maitre d', a token Portuguese of unblemished descent who was, as usual, anxious to stay in the good graces of those he'd risen above on the wings of short-lived concern for the 1,208 people of Portuguese descent on the island, accepted the question gracefully, with a small bow and quickly sought out the Senior Waiter. The Senior Waiter, who made it his business to know all things concerned with the hotel and its guests, did not have to summon junior waiters who scurried from dining room to dining room and dashed up and down the halls fulfilling requests for room service. They would have had to question, in addition to each other, the sanitation people and perhaps the laundry folk, the maids and janitors and the pool boys. The Senior Waiter did not have to go through that; nor did he have to play the fool for one of those security people, all of whom were from the United Kingdom, all poor and coarse and fighting tooth and nail to be accepted as Status Berhamians, at least, and never having to return home. They never knew anything. It took them a week to decipher notice of clothing lost in the laundry, and three months to admit they could not find the garment.

No. The Senior Waiter had the answer. For Mr. Frithe, but of course. The answer had come from the laundry room, though at that time it was simply information, which floated through the hotel every minute of the day, like wayward ghosts. Now standing at attention before the Maitre 'd, he sent the answer quivering back along the grapevine to where Frithe waited.

Fern Cromwell was indeed upstairs in her room at this very moment, recovering from a pussy-eating administered by old Bertram Neverson, conducted 90 minutes ago, and also recuperating from multiple scratches and two black eyes given her by Assistant Manager Sinclair Archibald last evening. The Management, knowing nothing of these activities, of course expects Mr. Archibald to be at his post at the usual hour—four this afternoon.

Laughing, Frithe rode away. Sinclair, he imagined, was still curled into a corner of the stone house, seeing his neck being fitted into a noose. Frithe would get back to him in a couple of hours.

For weeks now, perhaps because of the onset of summer with its pressing humidity, or because of the increase in tourists who brought with them the unending particles of newnesses from the outside world—the new songs, the latest disco steps, the smartest in clothing fashions—Cynthia Archibald, the former Miss Berhama, had been restless, narcotized as well by the unending dullness of her life.

She was, of course, married to a handsome assistant manager of the Queen whose future was assured, although no one knew just how brightly. They had a son as handsome as his father, and maybe moreso because he had his mother's fair skin. Cynthia's family, it was told on the island, was related and not so distantly, to the MacKenzies of Camelot Town. Not that it mattered as a rule; it was only when a Berhamian began to rise above the pack that his antecedents, often of ill-repute, were noised about.

They had a nice house, a very nice house for a young couple. Naturally, it was not close to the water; the whites had all those places. Nor did their house have an abundance of trees. It did have a view of the ocean, all of it, centered as it was on a hill in mid-island. The house baked in the summer and in winter was ravaged by the north winds.

Cynthia's glance fell on the powder blue Triumph that sat in the driveway, still shaking off dust from the trip to her mother's to leave Ralston. She had not told her mother about Sinclair's absence; she had been warned.

Still, this was the first time it'd happened since their marriage, and it was puzzling because she never believed that he would revert to his old ways. But Cynthia was not altogether unhappy. There had been times during their two years when she wished that she had not given herself, her life, her career up to a native Berhamian whose life was circumscribed by everything Berhamian. Two years of marriage had not, after all, cleansed her eyes of star dust.

This morning, then, sitting with a view of the driveway and the ocean north of the island, she smoked a long menthol cigarette and slowly sipped her coffee. Cynthia Archibald, studying her long, beige-colored (from the sun) legs—the way they widened at her thighs until her shorts pressed gently into them—tossed her long, brown hair. She was not unhappy. Her husband's overnight absence gave her the reasonable excuse, she told herself, to end her marriage.

She had read in her mother's paper that Sandy Lapidus had arrived on the island the day before yesterday to make final preparations for the appearance of his client, Jax Bendersen. Cynthia had met Lapidus in New York at the peak of her triumphal tour as Miss Berhama. Bendersen had not been his client then. Since then, however, he had acquired a host of rock stars and become famous.

"Anytime," Lapidus had breathed as they stood on the balcony of his room at the Plaza, still sipping Pol Rogét champagne, vintage 1968. "Anytime, babes, you want to do show biz big, look me up. I *will* be waiting."

She had done two years her parents' way, the Berhamian way. She'd come back to lend the aura of her name, her reputation to the Island, to encourage the youngsters. And she had been in love with Sinclair. "But dull," she said aloud, mashing out her cigarette carefully. "Dull as a bitch."

Cynthia reached decisively for the phone and dialed the Queen Hotel. When she heard the hello on the other end, she said, "This is Cynthia Manley, Sandy. Are you still waiting?"

Sandy Lapidus felt infinitely better when he hung up. He had been in a foul mood. He had not, as he had planned to, scheduled time to lie in the sun or to play tennis. He was nervous and afraid, and that had started at the airport.

"The Berhama Government wishes to advise all visitors that the importation of drugs is forbidden. The detection of narcotics by the police is subject to punishment. However, if you wish to turn in any drugs you may be carrying on your person or in your luggage, no penalty will follow."

The recording played every minute. Lapidus saw some young people, as if in shock, easing toward trash cans and dumping their grass, at which point, as though having watched from a secret place, the police suddenly appeared and carried the youngsters away.

Then there were the people who, deciding to work within the law, had voluntarily turned over their grass to the customs officials. They, too, had been led away protesting.

"Read this," a customs official had told Lapidus. Lapidus read the card which bore the same message that had been carried over the loudspeaker.

"Do you understand it, Sir?"

"Of course, I understand it," Lapidus said.

"How long are you here for, Sir?"

"About a week."

"I see. Open your bag, Sir."

"What?"

"Open your bag, Sir."

Lapidus was still remembering. No one had hipped him that Berhama was that way. Suppose he had been holding?

Agent agrees to provide at all times all services pertaining to the successful performances and well-being of the Artist, and to provide such services whenever and wherever requested.

Including dope, Lapidus now thought. And dope was what Bendersen was waiting for. It was to be delivered by Graham Rattery, a classmate and college radical turned farmer. Or so Lapidus thought. He didn't ask questions. Graham would deliver a quarter-pound of snort for Jax, his sidemen and friends. There were always friends. And he, Lapidus, would lay on Rattery $50,000 which would trickle somehow through the Berhama washing machine, he supposed, ending up almost anywhere in the world. They laundered money in Berhama, he had been told, with great efficiency and decorum—a certain *noblesse oblige* of which only the British-like functionaries were capable. Next to Switzerland, this was the next best place for such financial cleaning; forget Mexico, forget Lebanon.

Lapidus picked up the phone again and shifted the hour when he would meet with the manager of the Berhamian Royal Hotel and the electricians. He showered and doused himself liberally with cologne and powder, then eased himself into the $350 safari suit he'd had very painstakingly made of pima cloth dyed Miami Dolphin blue. It would be fitting for their rendezvous at Dolphin Bay. Lapidus struck two or three poses before the mirror, liked what he saw and grinned at himself. He was ready.

He passed through the *QE II* suite once more. It would satisfy Jax. Plenty of space, good view, solitude if he wished it. Only Lapidus' rooms (the B suite) and a smaller suite, the A, were on the floor. He'd done a good job. Jax wouldn't mind Cynthia's hanging around. Lapidus, however, didn't want Cynthia to take things seriously. The name of the game was jive; have a good time, then move on out. Pity she didn't have any talent—not the kind that would take her anywhere, really. Well, Lapidus, humming, closed the door, then bounced his way to the elevator, hearing one of Jax's tunes blasting inside his head.

The L2A1 Offensive Hand Grenade has an L25A4 fuse and is in service with the United Kingdom Forces. It replaces the 36 Defensive Hand Grenade, also known as the Mills Bomb or Grenade. Its design is effective, robust and modern. The outer cover is composed of thin sheet-steel, and it holds a coil of notched wires which fragment into predictable sizes. The fuse which has 4.3 sec delay, screws into the top of the body, thus affording a degree of safety. 25 meter radius.

New York, Texas, Providence and New York again. Wherever he went, Graham Rattery thought about the hand grenades which Peter Frithe by now would have received in the last shipment. And by the time he got back, the shipment of onion bulbs, Bermuda onion bulbs now grown in Texas, would be sitting in his small warehouse with its cargo of cocaine hidden in it. The drug would be converted into cash for Peter who, lukewarm about the project from the beginning, now seemed committed.

Rattery had had to get the coke in New York,

then trip to Texas for the bulbs. Then he had gone to Providence for a round of parties a few days before the race began. He did not expect to see many of them ever again. He wondered what Sandy would think if he knew. Lapidus seemed to have admired him during college. He had not registered surprise when Rattery contacted him to offer to supply Bendersen on his next trip Berhama. Maybe all former radicals were in that business now. Rattery wasn't, not for real; he was still radical, perhaps more than ever. He thought of the gathering that would take place on the lawn of the RBH. People still thought about the $250 million represented by the guests who went down with the *Titanic*, Rattery thought. Times had changed. The rich who raced their yachts and gathered in Berhama were worth billions. They wouldn't be worth much afterward, though. Rafferty was still surprised that some enterprising terrorist organization had not landed in Berhama, blown up the computers, snatched company officers and otherwise disrupted, at least for a time, the fast flow of capital from one end of the world to the other. Rafferty thought highly of himself for having conceived of this idea.

The Ratterys once had been a part of "The Group." (He still thought of them as such. The term lent a sinister seriousness to their arrangement, while "Dock Street Gang," bandied about by cab drivers and porters and the like, indicated less serious motives.) But over the years when the

73

members of "The Group" teamed up with each other, the Raffertys were always left out. And since these joinings were backed by double or triple or even quadruple the money the Ratterys possessed, which meant more staying power in every crisis, the Raffertys soon found themselves forced to seek aid from those who were squeezing them out of their middle-level mercantile ventures.

So small a place as Berhama could contain only so many such establishments—which all in "The Group" well knew. The Ratterys' request for help was refused. Politely, of course, and with regret. To cut losses, "The Group" offered them twenty cents on the dollar for stock and stores. By the time the Raffertys finished casting about for help elsewhere, in Canada and in the United Kingdom, "The Group," eager to divide the spoils, and sensing the kill, actually, knowing it, for they all had the same contacts all over the world, offered now ten cents on the dollar, and the Ratterys folded. They had only from "The Group" the assurance that the Rattery children naturally would have the education and opportunities anyone from their class had. There must be division between *them* and the *others*. Always. And good educations off the island were mandatory for the success of those divisions.

The Ratterys retired to their cottage, "The Group" devoured their holdings, dividing and sub-dividing them, and Graham Rattery was sent away to

America for his education, entering Cornell University the year after the black students walked out of Straight Hall with their shotguns and bandoliers. He was uneasy with the white students; and the black students, with whom he thought he might become friendly, rejected his advances, calling him "Honky" to his face. In the isolation of the bleak, snow-belted campus, with students occasionally splattering themselves upon the rocks 300 feet below the Suspension Bridge, Rattery reflected on the fate of himself and his family.

They had been oppressed. Just like the Blacks, the Indians, the Chicanos—just like everyone who, during that time, found ready audiences and cadres to listen to grievances. But why? They had been a part of "The Group." Why had they turned on them? Was it simply because of money?

In spite of the fact that the legends and jokes about Scots penuriousness and greed had been for a quarter of a century buried under nigger jokes, Jew jokes and Polish jokes, Rattery knew that the reality still existed. He would not know until he returned home that their banishment from "The Group" also had to do with his mother's refusal, while still unmarried, to wed old man MacKenzie who, like a true Scot, never forgot a slight.

During summers, instead of returning home to Berhama, Rattery travelled, saw riots, ran from them, became politicized then radicalized and came to see that Berhama was but a microcosm of western civilization, itself a rotting mass of culture upon which were feeding the rich and powerful who were growing richer and more powerful every day.

Unlike other radicals he came to know, Rattery professed nothing aloud and very little privately. He stayed in America for graduate work and then returned home, knowledgeable of the earth, vegetation and the primacy of agriculture. He took over the last 20 acres of land left to the family and began to cultivate it. The farming acreage had shrunk drastically, and with it, farmers. Everything was brought in at exhorbitant prices. Hotels were going up all over, and also guest houses and private homes and clubs. Rattery thought it evil that an island so small should tolerate seven 18-hole golf courses while some of the people still lived in shanties behind the heart of downtown Wellington in a section the tourists never saw.

Quietly and with a purpose recognized by some of the Blacks he'd grown up with, Rattery moved to create an awareness among the younger population of what was being done to them. He was allowed to join the Rastafarians, though he simply could not see Haile Selassie as anything more than a short man who ruled a poor country. But he said nothing when the emperor vanished, never to be seen again. The Berhama Rastas, in any case, tended to be more apolitical than anything, needing not politics, but a group to belong to.

The Jamaicans who were now arriving daily in

Berhama, brought the necessary militance to the Rastas, wearing their black, green and red caps, painting their mopeds black, green and red, and dancing to Bob Marley's music.

For most of the young black Berhamians who'd never been off the island, Graham Rattery was the nearest thing to a revolutionary god. He had spoken to Cleaver and Angela Davis, had chatted with Dick Gregory and LeRoi Jones; he had been in riots, rallies and on picket lines.

Rattery had counseled support of the Peoples Berhama Party and had joined it himself. This move had brought him a flurry of invitations from members of "The Group" who, over lunches at private clubs always near bays filled with the boats of the members, queried him on his reasons for joining PBP and advised him to quit it. Rattery laughed at them until his father made him understand one night at dinner in the cottage that, such as they had—the cottage, the 20 acres with its small buildings, the stipend, the memberships in various clubs—would go if Rattery insisted on his PBP membership. *And* if he persisted in his relationships with the revolutionary blacks.

Rattery backed off, maintaining only his relationship with Peter Frithe, an outsider now like himself and the three young men who worked with him on the farm growing onions and lettuce and tomatoes. But the Christmas Riots (as they were called) of a year ago triggered him back into action.

For it was clear that unrest and dissatisfaction had gripped the people once again, and things would never go back to the days of patronage and pseudo-patronage, the days of universal servant mentality, the times of accepting what "The Group" was willing to let seep down to the people. Change was on the way and he, Graham Rattery, was going to help it come.

SIX

"The Dog & Pony went well," Mandarino was saying. "They loved it."

"They always do," Kevin Levy said. "They need constant reassurance that we're doing something. They don't understand the nature of the business."

"They're used to money," Mandarino said. "They do this or that and the response to what they do is to make more money. They can feel that, smell it. It's real. Well. We'll take another poll, but first let's get a piece in that goddamn rag about polls generally. Soften them up a bit."

"Got a sked for it?" Mike Brooks sat at the other

79

end of the table and the small stack of papers in front of him worried Manadarino.

"Uh, say November, okay?"

Brooks scribbled a note to himself.

"It would be good to check out the ratings, see if they've changed. Gotta watch that 11-point lead. Not much when you figure all the things that can happen before Trotts gets his party in a position to call the next election."

Manadarino said, "Yeah. Right." He leaned forward on the table and looked north along Third Avenue, as he started to speak. "You guys correct me if I'm wrong, but I can't seem to get anything solid to hold onto with this Trottingham and his people." Now he looked at Levy and Brooks. "He told us that he wanted complete and total integration down 'ere; no bullshit about it. And that once he got that in order he was going to push for a black man to become the next Prime Minister—"

"No big thing, you know," Brooks said. "They've already had a black Prime Minister."

"What do you think, Mike, is he bullshitting?"

"You've been down there as often as I have."

"Kevin?" Mandarino asked, swinging away from Brooks.

For a moment they heard the hubbub of the office

outside—the typewriters, the phones, the copying machines, voices.

"He's a politician, like all the other politicians we've ever worked for," Levy said. "Why should we believe him and not the others?"

"Anthony Eden," Mandarino muttered.

"What?" Brooks said.

"I told him we'd make him another Anthony Eden."

"What'd he say?"

"He blushed—"

They laughed.

"—with pleasure."

"Did you finally give him the poll stats?" Levy asked.

"The stuff you gave me?"

"Yeah, the stuff I gave you." Levy came forward in his seat. "Not the raw stuff."

"No. God," Mandarino said. "If he only knew how close those other guys were he'd shit in his pants. Donnelly and DeSilva, 15 points ahead of him!"

"He's probably guessed that," Brooks said, "by the way we took so much time to caution him that,

81

if they were just a *little* ahead of him, they had no responsibility comparable to his. He knows. As a matter of fact, I got word this morning from there that he may shift his cabinet around, move those two threats to to where they won't get quite so much publicity."

"Who told you that?" Mandarino asked.

"Phipps, the Gossip."

"About how much of what he says is true?"

"Half."

Levy laughed. "So, it won't be both of them. Just one."

Brooks said, "He can't outright get rid of the black people in his cabinet; too much fuel for the Opposition. So, he'll shuffle 'em around."

"Did he say anything about the tourist business getting back to normal yet?"

Mandarino said, "Not yet, but it's better than it was. They think that by summer it'll be back to normal."

"Unless they have more riots this coming Christmas," Brooks said.

Mandarino thrust his chin at Brooks. "Okay, smart-ass, why should they riot again?"

Brooks grinned. "Thought you'd never ask." He

began to pick up the papers. Levy and Mandarino groaned. "Hey, look," Brooks said. "If you guys would read the fuckin' memos I give you you'd know as much as I did."

"C'mon, willya? I gotta see Senator Smitkin in twenty minutes."

"Didja know," Levy said, "one third of the U.S. Senate is composed of millionaires?"

"Good fuckin' thing," Mandarino said. "Or we'd be outa business. C'mon, Mike."

"They got it all wrong down there, Gary. You simply cannot expect successive generations of people to grow up knowing they'll be nothing more than servants to the world. They're awfully complacent about that."

"I know what you're saying," Mandarino said. "But is that really our concern?"

"Maybe not ours, Gary, but the people down there we work for, who want to win the next election so they can keep making money. Hey look, don't saddle me with that shit you're implying."

"What shit? What shit?" Mandarino leaned back from the table and stretched his arms imploringly to Levy.

"What I mean, Gary, is that these things impact on what we're trying to do. It's history. It's the way things are because no one wanted to make the changes back then. Now here it is. I'm giving you my best shots—"

"Okay, okay." Mandarino glanced at his watch.

"And the Reggae-Rasta kids know it," Brooks went on. "More than half the goddamn population down there is under twenty-five." Brooks leaned back. "They still got time to defuse the bomb." He discarded one paper and picked up another. "Do you know the price of food down there?"

Levy smiled and shook his head. They all stayed at the Queen, had unlimited room service, ate at the best restaurants and moved through Berhama on a fluff of expense accounts. "That's rhetorical," Brooks said. "A single potato costs 19 cents. To replace a car key costs four dollars—"

"Got it," Mandarino said.

"That $8,000 median wage they're always talking about isn't real—closer to $5,000, when you trade off the costs of things, and they're going up all the time, but they aren't getting anymore money to—"

"Gary—'scuse me, Mike," Levy said. "Did you get into that voluntary wage control thing with Trotts?"

Mandarino snapped his fingers. "Forgot, kid, but we'd better damned well keep that in mind. Does that go along with what you're sayin', Mike?"

"Yeah, it does. He'd better come out quick with

a companion piece: voluntary price controls. You
know what his trouble is, and the trouble with all
his people? They don't give those Blacks any credit
for being able to think!"

"What else, Mike?" Mandarino watched Levy
scribble.

"You really got to get on them for that Rhodesia
package."

"What the fuck's the Rhodesia package?" Mandarino looked from Brooks to Levy.

Levy said, "Those four laws that went through
this spring. Uh, increasing the size of the regiment,
the curfew, stepping up recruitment of cops from
the UK or Jamaica, permitting certain groups to
have weapons and rifle practice, and uh—"

"That's it," Brooks said.

Mandarino stroked his chin. "That your idea,
Mike, Rhodesia package?"

"Well—" Brooks grinned at Levy.

"He told me," Mandarino swung around to the
window again. "He told me that all they were using
with the rifle package were .22s."

"Our guys in Vietnam," Levy said, "were using
5.56 millimeter bullets. Standard now. And the Italians, Swiss, Israelis, French and Belgians use it."

"Kevin. What's your fuckin' point? I gotta go."

85

"I think," Brooks said, "Kevin was saying that that is close, very close, to .22s."

"No shit?"

"Gary, he may not know that," Brooks said.

Mandarino straightened. "What's the Opposition say? I mean, they got 18 guys in the Lower House. Didn't they raise a stink? How about that babe, the PBP leader?"

"Ida Jones-Williams. They haven't said anything, except about the curfew," Levy said.

Mandarino got up. "It could blow up, it could blow up. Anyway, you guys get together all the stuff we want to talk to Trottingham about. We can't let their thing go off in our faces, when our next stop could be Washington and Washington being interested in that little outpost. I don't want to have to start wiping off the eggs. See ya."

Levy said, "Why in the hell do we all have to go next week? I'm up to my ears with Governor Tate."

"Because Trotts wants us to catch the Providence–Berhama scene. 'For color,' he said. But also to let us know how many big bucks people hang out there."

"He's like year-old frozen fish," Levy said. "No vibes, not even a decent stink. I don't like him. I wanna stick it to him."

"If we do our job right, babes, he's gonna be stuck!"

Mandarino did not like the look and smell of it. Too many ragged edges. Trottingham played too many games, telling this one that, and that one this, and then denying it all, saying he had been misunderstood. A man that bright doesn't get misunderstood unless it's on purpose. What I ought to be doing, Mandarino thought, is working for the other side.

"Gary? Gary?" Don Hummerford, tall and thin, leaned into Mandarino's path as he walked through the office.

"Yeah, Don. I got a meeting right now and I'm late. Can yours wait a while?"

"Just wanted to let you know that those Berhama people haven't anted up in three months. That's all."

"Why didn't you tell me before?"

"Thought it was on the way."

"Listen, you call those pricks right now and tell them to come up with the bread before the week's out or we're walking and suing as well. Tell Kevin and Mike. I'll call down there when I'm finished."

Jesus Christ, Mandarino thought. Anyone of those guys could spit and hit a couple of million bucks. Fuckin' Scots. So goddamn tight they can make Indians on the old nickels straddle the buffalos. Mandarino smiled. His father used to say that.

87

He wondered how Suzanne Kendrick was. If not for her he would not be going down next week; to hell with it. Mike or Kevin or just one of them could go down. Trottingham should thank Sooz. What the hell did he, Mandarino, care about a goddamn yacht race? He got seasick taking a bath. Hey, he thought, entering his office where Senator Smitkin now stood with a smile, his hand extended, I should take her some dynamite gift, from Bloomie's maybe.

Dolphin Bay faced the east. The ocean rolled in warm and blue, and smashed itself against the long, wide shelf of sand and rock and rushed ashore in boiling foam. Now it was almost deserted. Suzanne Kendrick watched the movement of the sea, as hypnotized by it as though she were watching flames in a fireplace. She felt comfortable now. The few people who had passed her as she lay beneath her umbrella on her back, paid no attention other than what was usual; their eyes did not linger on her breasts for longer than the least ordinary visual caress.

She turned now so that she was facing up the beach and started to adjust her bathing suit. She stopped herself and let her fingers play near the top, at the V between the breasts. She watched the man in the blue safari suit walking arm in arm with the tall, attractive young woman. She had vaguely Negroid features, the woman, but she was so fair

88

that Suzanne could not be sure. She thought of them together, nude, the man fondling the young woman's breasts, kissing them, suckling them. She thought about such things all the time now.

Suzanne pressed her hand against the prostheses. This was the first time she'd worn them in a bathing suit. She turned back to the ocean over which Gary would come flying in a few days. What would his reaction be? Should she even—Well, why not? Why should she do without just because of a double mastectomy; she still had her needs, her desires. But, suppose when he saw he couldn't?

Oh, Suzanne thought, that would kill me, really kill me. She dug her toes into the sand. From under her sunglasses she looked up at the sky. Why, she said softly, why did you do this to me?

Kirkland Trottingham was still smarting from Mandarino's telephone call. No one had ever spoken to him like that, ever. He was just as upset about his own response which had been profusely apologetic. Closer to servile, he now thought. That Dago pipsqueak, talking to me like that, he thought. I never even let Italians clean my bathroom! His lips trembled. And the language. Not that I'm a prude, but gotdamn.

Trottingham straightened. Perhaps I should terminate the arrangement. He brightened. Then his mind touched on the ramifications of such an act.

Siggonson and the Opposition would make too much of it. He groaned into the emptiness of his office. If BUP couldn't get along with its own public relations consultant, how did it expect to continue to run Berhama? Gross incompetence. At the least, incompatibility. Trottingham of course had reprimanded Phipps, the Party treasurer, for failing to send the payments on schedule. But Phipps had countered in his insinuating way by saying that he, Trottingham, had failed to approve the checks when they were written.

Trottingham chewed at his lips. Of course, the fund to pay Mandarino and his people had been created at his bank where it drew interest at twelve per cent. It was not unusual to let a bill hang as long as possible before paying it so that the interest it was accruing, if such an arrangement had been made, could be used to pay off the principal. "O! I thought those checks were for something else," Trottingham had told Phipps. "Here, make out a new one for the total mount and I'll sign it immediately."

Phipps never tanned. He simply got red. Clever man, Trottingham thought, a real Scot.

Phipps knew that the difference between them was that, as far back as his family went, it was law-abiding. *His* forebears had not been rounded up as thieves and placed aboard ships going to Ogelthorpe or Berhama, or to Australia. He had come to Berhama voluntarily, after having served in the

South Atlantic during World War II aboard the destroyer, *Antelope.*

On this day, while Trottingham sat groaning into the silence of his office, Phipps sat in his, ten blocks away, thinking once again that the Prime Minister had dumped on him, as he invariably managed to dump on everyone he came in contact with. He thought back to the time, years ago in Glasgow, when a visiting American had remarked on the virtual nonexistence of crime in the country and asked why.

"My dear Sir," Phipps had said, "we got rid of our criminals a long time ago when we shipped them to America and elsewhere." And now the sons of sons of sons of sons of criminals were in charge in Berhama. Phipps snorted.

Trottingham was thinking, as he looked over his calendar, that it was unfortunate that Phipps knew his many failings, but there was nothing the man could do about it except to take orders as always, and to present himself as the sacrificial lamb whenever necessary. There was the unwritten rule that, if one did not play the game, one was sidelined—permanently. As for Mandarino, there was nothing to do except to tolerate his crudeness until they won the election. Then he'd tell him off. Spic. Rum drinker.

When the phone rang, Trottingham muttered, "All right, Talbot," and picked it up.

"Mr. Tannock to see you, Prime Minister." Amanda always spoke in low, leisurely voice, as though just waking up.

"Ah, yes. Send him on in."

Trottingham never knew what to do with his hands upon meeting people. People he saw often did not, he thought, require a handshake. And being the Prime Minister, he ought not to offer his hand first. He stood then, his hands tightly clasped atop his groin. He saw Tannock often enough since he was the Minister of Finance and ran seven departments.

"Hallo, Talbot. Sit down."

Talbot Tannock was a small, nervous man with a pinched face. He moved like a bird across a lawn. He made Trottingham nervous and that was why he wanted him to sit down. "Kirkland. Good to see you. I hope you have some real time for me this morning."

"Yes, yes, yes, Talbot. All the time you need, of course." Tannock did run the most important Ministry, even more important than Tourism, and he ran it well. He had been working on a scheme, so far hush-hush, to bring to Berhama some middle-of-the-road project, something not quite as risky as the gambling in the Bahamas and not quite as dull as what Bermuda had, which was nothing much. Something to take up the slack when tourism went into its downcurve. Tannock worked very hard. It was his brainchild that had brought all the foreign Exempted Companies to Berhama which had made the members of "The Group" ever more wealthy. But Tannock had said over the phone that he wished to talk about one of those very companies.

Tannock squared his shoulders. "Kirkland, the Mounties are here."

Trottingham tilted his head. "Mounties? The Royal Canadian Mounted Police?"

"Yes, that's right."

"But why?"

"You'll know soon enough. Rad Limited, that Ottawa-based company? Seems they've been charged with some sort of fraud in Canada and two constables arrived here last night for the purpose of investigating the Rad Limited records down here."

Trottingham got up quickly. "Oh, I see." He sat down again, crossing one of his legs, and flicked his foot up and down, staring stonily at his Minister of Finance. "Well, we can't have that, can we, Talbot?"

"Well, Kirkland—"

"What's their procedure?"

"They'll make application directly to you to be allowed to search the premises of Rad Limited."

"I'll refuse permission, of course."

"Then they will go to our courts."

"Naturally."

"Where, I imagine, proceedings will take long enough for them to put their business in order."

"Exactly, Talbot. As long as these companies behave themselves in Berhama, we'll protect them. But really, we do want class companies, you know; none of those fly-by-night operators. And nothing like that Robert Vesco, with half the American agencies running after him."

"I agree, Kirkland, and we do try, of course, to license only the highest caliber companies."

"Umm," Trottingham said, making a great effort not to look at his watch. "So," he said. "So." He flicked his foot again.

"One of our friends in the London business circle tells me not to be surprised if we receive notice of a pending visit from the King of Abu Dabi." Tannock smiled brightly.

Trottingham stopped flicking his foot and gripped the sides of his chair. "Is that right? Humm." He leaned back in his chair. "Talbot, you do have time for a cup of tea, don't you?"

"Yes, Sir, I do."

With a bound, Trottingham was at his desk

phoning his secretary. "Do bring in some tea for us, Amanda. Thank you." Smiling, Trottingham regained his seat. "Would you have any idea, Talbot, why the king of Abu Dabi would want to visit Berhama? Should it be a state visit, state dinner, red carpet, evening dress and all that? What do you think, Talbot?"

Tannock smiled to himself, then said, "I would suppose His Majesty is looking around for investments."

But Trottingham wasn't listening to him. His hands were folded and his head lifted upwards; his eyes were on the ceiling of his office, envisioning, Tannock knew, all manners of deals, lucrative to be sure, in which he could involve himself. "Do you know if Arabs like black people, Talbot?"

Surprised, Talbot Tannock straightened in his own chair. "Why, I really don't know, Kirkland. It is my impression that many Arabs are black."

"Yes, yes, I suppose. Hummm. The king of Abu Dabi." Trottingham smiled and rose to take the tea tray from Amanda. As he sat the tray down and gestured to Tannock to pour his own, Trottingham said, "When would this be, do you think?"

Laughing, Tannock said, "Well, if we manage to survive the bloody yacht race, sometime the week after."

"That doesn't give us too much time. But we'll manage."

SEVEN

One hundred and seventy yachts had gathered on Rhode Island Sound, and they bobbed and dipped in the soft, long swells that curled in from the ocean, and the wind ran around their brightly colored, now reefed, sails; the sun, curving down the southwest sky, was fast losing its heat. Aboard the ships, the Moody's and Verls, the Holmatics and Condors, the Voyagers and Ericsons, the Oysters and Swans, the captains and crews studied the surface and weather reports passed on by the director of the Woods Hole Oceanographic Institution and the young meteorologist from the U.S. National Weather Service.

For the next twelve hours they had been told, they could expect 8–10 knot southeasterly winds. They could not anticipate too much assistance from the Gulf Stream because it was swinging too far to the east. But they could expect a 15–24 knot breeze once they got on the rhumb line that ran from where they were anchored directly to Berhama.

The briefings finished, the crews went ashore for dinner. In the morning, with the firing of the gun, they would begin their race 635 miles over the open sea.

"They're on the way!" All over Berhama the word went. Money would flow like water when the ships came in. There would be endless parties. Cab drivers, waiters, bartenders would rake in the tips. Hotels would have no vacancies; indeed, Sinclair Archibald had just informed a caller from New York that the Queen was full. The last three rooms had been booked by Mandarino Associates, one of several firms for which the Queen always had rooms available. The owner of the hotel, Archibald knew, was a prominent officer in the BUP and The Dock Street Gang. Such arrangements were standard all over Berhama.

The desk was quiet now. Archibald telephoned 1020. "How are you?" he asked without preliminary. At first there was silence, but it was followed by a low, lilting chuckle.

"Not as much of a mess as I was three days ago."

Archibald turned from the phone and exhaled long and cautiously. "I'm glad," he said. "And I'm sorry. Very sorry."

"So am I. I decided to stay longer—the black eyes and the scratches, you know."

"I'm sorry, darling."

There was another silence. "Darling? Are you drunk, Sinclair?"

Archibald laughed. "No, not at all."

"Isn't your wife putting out?"

Archibald laughed again. Not only was she not putting out, she had moved to her mother's. "Sure, she is," he lied. "But I've had a chance to do some thinking—about uh, arrangements, you know, if you've forgiven me."

"Say no more. I'm here until the yacht race."

"Good. When may I see you, Fern?"

"Give me one more day, my man, and you got a deal."

"Can I send you up anything?"

"Just yourself. Tomorrow. Tomorrow night. Is that all right?"

"Well—look, I thought you might be interested in a story."

"This whole damned place is a story, if I could just pull it together."

"You knew about Jax Bendersen?"

"The rock star? No. That's not much of a story, my dear."

"Oh, well." Archibald had thought that he might lead Cromwell to the man who had been seeing his wife, Bendersen's agent, he had been told. Then perhaps, Fern might lead him away with her bubbling charms and he might be able to recapture Cynthia. He needed her if he was to maintain the proper front for getting ahead. Or, he thought as he whispered goodbye to Cromwell, he needed someone else. Let the bellmen and waiters, the laundry people, the maids and janitors, give him those quick, knowing looks; they would always be what they were. He was going to continue upward. He knew when they were out of his earshot they laughed about him and how his woman had taken herself a man; not any old man, but a white man. An *important* white man. It was necessary to make that qualification, for they all knew white men who were not any more important than they. But it galled Archibald to know that the man was in the hotel. And he knew that Cynthia dared not come to him here. But hotels, he thought, were as numerous as the blades of grass.

He picked up the ringing phone. "Desk, Mr. Archibald. May I help you?"

99

"Tomorrow, my dear. But now, are you holding a reservation for a Gary Mandarino?"

"Why, yes. Uh, how did you know? It's Mr. Mandarino," he said, shuffling through the reserve cards, "Mr. Levy and Mr. Brooks."

"Mike Brooks? Kevin Levy?"

"That's right."

"Uh-huh! For when?"

"Next Monday."

"When the ships are due?"

"Yes. They're due the day after."

"Ah, thank you, Sinclair. Tomorrow, then." She made kissing sounds. Archibald smiled and hung up.

"You heard that?"

Linda Churchill nodded.

Cromwell pointed a finger at her. "All right now. You'll do for your outfit and I'll do for mine. No conflict." She got up to fix more drinks. Once, she reflected as she looked at Churchill, I looked as good as that. Shit, better.

Cromwell gave Churchill the vodka and ginger. She couldn't get over it, though. Vodka and ginger ale. Why was it that people in the tropics always messed up their drinks. Scotch and ginger. But then, she thought, she knew people who drank scotch and sweet milk, and gin and coke.

Cromwell smiled. "So, you don't want to tell me who told you I was here?"

"No." Churchill smiled. "I have my sources."

"Yes," Cromwell said, drinking, "Don't we all."

"But you have yours where it, or they, count. And I have mine."

"Then your source knew why I was holed up here in my room?"

Churchill inadvertantly spat up a part of her drink as she laughed. "Yes!"

For a moment Cromwell was indignant. Then she started to laugh, too. "Listen," she said. "Have you ever laid the Prime Minister?"

"Trottingham?" Churchill pronounced it Trottinghummmm. "No. As a matter of fact, it has never crossed my mind. He's a most unappetizing man . . ." She seemed to be thinking about it. "No," she said with some finality. "No, I simply wouldn't do it."

Cromwell, laughing, leaned forward. "Listen, little sister, just what the hell's going on around here?"

Of the 20 Parliamentarians on the Government/Berhama United Party side of the House, not including the Prime Minister and the Speaker, Roi Donnelly and Luis DeSilva were the stars of the front bench. There were many and frequent complaints in Berhama about the inferior quality of the House. Decorum had vanished; eloquence slept; debating skills were better used in Wellington Market; sensible speech had gone on an extended vacation—and no one knew when it would return.

Of course, behind the complaints lay the whispered laments from both black and white Berhamians, that the composition of the house no longer was all white and therefore could not possibly reflect the majesty of the British heritage they seemed so proud of.

Berhamians assumed, as most people do, that their representatives in Government were honest, capable and at the very least intelligent enough to make a point or two during the time when Parliament was in session. In Berhama the Ministers and other Parliamentarians held their offices but part-time. The salaries were correspondingly meagre. The capable people, it was readily acknowledged, were too rich to accept full-time offices; they would have turned them down out of hand. The clods on the whole were eager to accept full-time offices along with full-time salaries.

Donnelly and DeSilva were the only exceptions to the rule. They were not terribly rich but they were terribly capable. Nor were they "welfare cases," Ministers or Parliamentarians so poor that The Dock Street Gang had to provide jobs for them befitting their status as officers of the nation of Berhama.

Roi Donnelly, like Luis DeSilva, was an attractive man. He owned the Berhamian equivalent of Col. Saunders Kentucky Fried Chicken, with branches in each of the nineteen districts: *Donnelly's Delightful Chicken.*

Upon his small fleet of Datsun station wagons, Donnelly had mounted large cut-outs of chickens (Roosters), and these, rushing to and from deliveries, did for Donnelly what no public relations firm, including Mandarino Associates, could do for his image. When he rose to his feet in the House, slowly, every fold in his Saville Row suit whispering richly, the people in the small gallery, even the tourists, were arrested by his movements which embodied a kind of majesty anthropologists never seem to discover in people darker than themselves. Across the House, the Opposition stilled in its motions, which somehow seemed to be related in imagery to the movements black people are reported to have on Saturday nights in certain decrepit neighborhoods.

None of that movement from the Bench to the adjoining Rooms for a quick nip for Donnelly. Beginning with an innocuous, shadowy *basso profundo*, he moved in on the Opposition—seemingly in retreat—while his flanks encircled, a classical manueveur called The Double Envelopment, used successfully at Cannae by Hannibal and by Shaka and Umpanda against the British and the Boers in Southern Africa.

A fact here, a fact there, an apparent stumble in logic. Recovery. Apology, but with reservations and then, miraculously, these stopped coming; the random facts were hooked together, tightened, the noose drawn and Donnelly had won another debate for Government. Scorn, contempt, derision, bombast (when he was sure and in a great hurry), all were a part of his arsenal.

Out of the House he was gracious and charming and deadly lecherous; he drank a good drink, laughed a lot and was generous; he leaked important information to his favorite reporter, Linda Churchill who, after all, fucked well for a cockney and, what else was there to do on Berhama to keep amused but to play games with people and situations?

At the moment, Roi Donnelly was sprinkling his scrotum generously with Yves St. Laurent talcum powder. He splashed his favorite scent, Royal Lyme Lotion, over the rest of his body. Tonight he was meeting Fern Cromwell who would also entertain his colleague, Minister Without Portfolio for Information, the Hon. Luis DeSilva, and his very good friend, Linda Churchill. It promised to be a rare evening. It also held great possibilities that he might be seen one day on American television.

Luis De Silva had had a reputation as a cocksman mainly because he himself talked constantly about getting laid. He talked of the tourists he'd made, visiting female celebrities, women he'd met in Lisbon, New York and London. For a quarter of a century DeSilva had talked of getting laid. But no one had ever seen him with any woman other than his wife. DeSilva had talked for so long and so often about his feats that people tired of deriding him, and let him talk.

Like everyone else in Parliament, he wished to know Linda Churchill better. It sometimes seemed to him that she had been to bed with every member of the House but him. Vanity, however, would not let him believe that.

He, too, as Donnelly had, made some excuse for having to go out. A meeting. And smelling as sweetly as Donnelly, although his scents ran to the Portuguese or Spanish, DeSilva drove whistling to the Queen hotel where he would meet his colleague, Roi, the famous Fern Cromwell and Linda Churchill. He might even wind up on American television. And when that segment of what he assumed would be Fern Cromwell's newscast was relayed to Berhama, he would be even more popular than at present.

105

His style in the House ran to the American—he had always admired American politicians, especially those from the South. Whenever he spoke a southern accent crept inexplicably into his pronounciation. He was a good speaker, but a more effective wheeler dealer in the image of Lyndon Baines Johnson. If some legislation was having a rough go of it, he was the man who soothed his own side of the House and then soothed, cajoled or threatened the Opposition.

Luis DeSilva owned three supermarkets, the most elegant in Wellington, of course, specializing in French products. In the others he could be seen from time to time working on the cash registers or packing meat, or pushing wagons filled with cartons of milk. DeSilva liked to be seen in the role of commoner—especially in the parishes where all were commoners—talking and joking with the people. Invariably his topics with the men ran to church and pussy, tourists and pussy, the Opposition and pussy, the weather and pussy, inflation and pussy and, because he considered himself to be good with his fists, fighting and pussy. The black people who shopped in the two markets outside Wellington liked him because he was vociferous in his dislike of The Dock Street Gang of which he was not a member—no Portuguese was—though he wished he were. He was that new man, symbolic of the coalition of blacks and Portuguese who one day would overcome the establishment.

As for his unverified conquests of women—well,

one had to do *something* on Berhama, and DeSilva's thing was less harmful than many others'.

In Cromwell's suite, Churchill was supplying, as she drank vodka and ginger ale, a briefing in preparation for their evening's activities: "We can count on their having had a few drinks. They hold their liquor well until about 8:30. They have a tendency to waste time by complaining about the Prime Minister—that's kind of a past-time here, in case you've forgotten." Churchill had gone to her apartment and changed. Cromwell, with her dark glasses on, looked almost normal.

Cromwell nodded. "Which one do you want?"

"Ugh. Neither, but I suspect that DeSilva would have an interest in you. And Donnelly's an old habit of mine. Okay?"

"I don't care. Maybe we shouldn't have dinner here at the hotel, right?"

"Right. I made a reservation at the Caribbean Star. Sort of French, very exclusive. I got a chalet." That's a small, private room, about the most private kind of place you can get on Berhama."

"Expensive?"

"Very. But these honorable gentlemen have money, and they like exclusive places and people, and they're going to like us."

"Who in 'The Gang,' " Cromwell asked, "owns this restaurant?"

Churchill laughed. "Trottingham."

"They own everything," Cromwell muttered. "People, too."

"You must have guessed that over the years you've been coming down here."

Cromwell sighed. "Didn't bother. What got me started was seeing Mandarino here and where he is, something big's going on and I need an offbeat story, especially with this prolonged vacation."

They heard masculine voices in the hall and then a knock.

Churchill said, "Fern, it's time to go to work."

"You seem a bit down, my darling," Gretta Trottingham said to her husband. They were alone in the house. It was a rare evening when it was so.

"Oh, just one of those days when I got bloody tired of it all, Grettie. MacKenzie's been snapping at my heels like the shaggy old dog he is. That Italian fellow, Mandarino, is getting damned snippy. Phipps' insinuations are becoming intolerable—it's not what he says or even what he does; it's *how* he does things. And those bloody reporters of Siggonson's. And Donnelly and DeSilva—you know, I bet those clods got more points than I did in that survey that Italian conducted. I must put it to him when he's down. But, hah! I don't bloody care what they got. Can you imagine a chicken dealer running this government? Or a gotdamn supermarket clark? People don't know when they're well off."

"Don't upset yourself, Kirkland."

"I'm not upset. I'm furious. I'd like to take a good vacation, but how can I leave the country in the hands of the deputy Prime Minister, that ass? Or all those others next in line in seniority? This place would disintegrate without me running it." Trottingham paused to take several deep breaths. "Clods, all of them! And to think that some of them have bigger houses than we do, struggling with mortgages to be sure, and not that I give a damn. Swimming pools bigger than ours, two tennis courts—bloody gotdamn baboons."

Greta Trottingham rose quietly and began to clear the table. She moved back and forth between the dining room and the kitchen like a shadow, while her husband sat staring out across the bay.

"And dear old Douglas MacKenzie has been slipping money to the Opposition—buying insurance just in case they win. That ass over at the U.S. Consulate wants to get together to discuss the election—alternatives, he said, in case BUP loses. You know what that bloody well means, don't you? Their wretched CIA, those bloody bumblers. And the Mounties are here, and the king of Abu Dabi is looking for investments on the island, and DeSilva and Donnelly are up to something, I know it, and now this bloody gotdamn yacht race! And can you believe it—people are advising me to take on Peter Frithe as a board member of the bank. It would quiet the Opposition, they say, if we take on that broken former union ass. God, I am fed up!"

"I got an invitation to speak at a church today," Greta Trottingham said. "Shall I accept?" She had moved out of the room before Trottingham could answer.

When she returned he said, "I would imagine that's precisely what Mandarino wants, my dear. And that reminds me of the House, oddly enough. You'd think it was some kind of pool hall the way they carry on in there. Disgraceful. Reminds me of that time we went to one of their churches. Sat through that three-hour sermon, and at the end of it, what carryings-on! Dancing, clapping, shouting, sweating—good Lord! I won't have to go will I?"

His wife laughed and patted his shoulders. "No, Kirkland. I can manage."

He reached and took her hands. "I wish very often these days that I hadn't taken this job."

"Just today," she said. "And other days. It's natural. But Kirkland, you know you wanted it and would have died if they hadn't offered it to you."

Trottingham stilled. "Who else was there? Who? Tell me?"

Greta Trottingham slipped her hands into his. "Someone always rises to the occasion. Sometimes, Kirkland, you greatly underestimate people."

"Nonsense!" Trottingham said, standing abruptly. "I know all these people and they would not have been worth two hoots in hell. We'd be floundering in a disaster right now, right now, I tell you, if I hadn't been available."

Greta Trottingham sighed. "As you wish." She smiled brightly. "What shall we do? What would you like to do to take your mind off that filthy old job?"

"Something exciting," he said.

"Yes, you cold fish, of course, something exciting."

Trottingham became petulant. "I really don't like for you to say that. You know it leaves uh, uh, bad image, as it were." Berhamians pronounced "were" like "ware."

"Sorry, darling. Come, what shall we do? Liven up the place."

"I've got it. Let's play darts." He strode toward the den.

With the night settling in, the southwest sky a parabola of blues, purples and reds, Peter Frithe walked slowly along Dock Street. As long as he could remember there were the ships. And now they loomed, different ones to be sure, up into the night sky at the very center of Dock Street, their riding lights on, their deck lights blazing. He loved the very stink of their salted steel hulls and the way they seemed to make the water smell when they were tied up. Here and there on the invariably white hulls he could see rust marks. He paused before the *Rotterdam*. How many places had it been to, he wondered. How many more places would it go to? There it was, huge, inanimate, yet it had gone to places he had only dreamed of, perhaps 200 times. He felt no envy, just a vague sense of pride that it had done so without any loss of life. As long as there was life, one had to have some hope.

Frithe sat down at the edge of one of the docks and let his feet dangle over the edge. The overhang of a light allowed him to see irridescent ripples moving secretly between the ship and the street wall. He watched them, marvelling that driplets of oil, cast down into a corner filled with debris, produced such color.

And now he heard the sound of the horses and carriages, the night transport for young lovers and elderly people who still loved each other and, perhaps, a remembered way of travelling. Frithe rose and moved again along the street, walking slowly and in the shadows. He was not hiding. In Berhama

112

everyone knew just about everyone else and he, surely, was very well known, even in his banishment. That became an example, if one did not work well with the team. Tonight, just for a few moments, he wanted to be alone.

Passing across the street from the Dock Street Disco where the tourists were flocking in, he was haunted, but just for a moment, by graceful movements of the dancers, often stilled by strobes, and by the music that was pounding through the building. All was watched, of course, by the big, neatly dressed bouncers. The tourists must be made safe; harm to them meant harm to the economy and harm to each and every Berhamian. Too often it seemed that the government paid more care to the tourists than it did to its citizens.

He paused in his walk before Luis DeSilva's *French Gourmet*. One of the few Portuguese who'd made it; most of the rest were still gardeners or waiters. Those who'd risen through the ranks of the hotel workers to become head waiters had done so through the connivance of The Dock Street Gang: a wedge, a buffer, between themselves and the black Berhamians. He had told his union members that. It was not that they hadn't listened; they simply could not afford to do what he advised.

But it was all all right now. Frithe didn't wish to destroy anything, let alone people. He was a builder, or had been. He had finally been forced to think of himself and he had put his six month's stint in the U.S. Army at Ft. Bragg to use. He wondered how many young Berhamians these days were seeking papers through the U.S. Consulate to join the U.S. Army. Well, if he hadn't gotten out with a medical discharge, he would not have gone to hotel school and his life would have been nothing.

There were two new interior decorating stores on Dock Street. They were filled with soft lights, expensive furniture and furnishings—American style. His own apartment was threadbare and unkempt and dark, even on days when the sun shone brightest.

He passed the Cabinet Building where some tourists were gathered, watching the Regiment in bright red uniforms performing evening colors. Frithe passed another disco, a local one, where few white people went. The Queen Hotel towered above the trees ahead of him. He would go in and chat with Sinclair if he was not busy. As he headed up the walk to the hotel, he wondered how Graham Rattery would take it when it all came down front. He would be angry, but maybe he would be relieved, too. Rattery was a Berhamian. Yet, he had seen to the delivery of the grenades.

And he had planned the manner in which they were to be used. Frithe had concealed his shock and slowly came to realize that they, Dock Street, "The Group," had injured the Ratterys far more than he would ever allow them to hurt him.

"Peter."

"Hello, hello," he responded to the cab drivers parked in the lot.

"Long time no see, boy, how you keepin'?"

"Steady, steady."

"Evenin', Peter."

"Hello, James."

Waiting. Some of the drivers had spent most of their adult lives waiting for fares: waiting for someone to want them. Had waited to be spoken to, had waited for payment, hoping for a tip: had waited, even, to be called, to be recognized. That was Berhama's fate. Now something was quickening inside Frithe, a rising hunger, a restlessness he understood too well.

"Hey," he said to Archibald. "You all right?"

Archibald grinned sheepishly. "Yes, man, thank the Lord. And Fern's not mad."

"Got around to callin her, did you?"

"Had to call somebody since Cynthia's gone."

"Talked to her?"

"Every day. Five, six times a day. The answer is no."

"Ah well, Sin. When this man tells her to meet

115

him at the airport for the flight to New York, and tells her he will have her ticket, and that she should meet him for the 8 P.M. plane, and she goes, my man, decked out like the Miss Berhama she was, having left your son with her momma, she will find that he's not there; that he left on the 6 P.M. plane, and she'll come back. They always do."

"Yes, I suppose. Want to run tonight? Go somewhere and get stinking hot?"

"Yes, Sin, I would like very much to do that, and I would also like some pussy. So I will be back at midnight when you will have finished your tour."

"Right on, Peter."

EIGHT

Saturday morning. The rising sun glistened on the spray-dampened spinnakers which represented every color known, every color dreamed of. One hundred and seventy hulls of sloops and yachts strained against the endless clutch of the sea. Wood and fibreglass, with sails of Terylene or canvas, with ropes of hemp or nylon, the vessels knifed on, their crews awakening with the brightening sun. The ships bore names like *Smokey Bear*, *Evita*, *Iberian Shamrock*, *Indulgence*; and *Battlecry*, *Saracen*, *Acadia*, *Tenacious*; and *Lady Mine*, *Bravura*, *Tempest* and *Seabird*, and a hundred more. On they came, pouring on the sail to catch the morning's

117

wind, up eight knots from the evening before. Like the judgment day of brightly-colored birds, they fanned out upon the sea, crashing and burning, moving down the rhumb line away from the American coast to the open, ever-bluing ocean to Berhama.

Graham Rattery, the same day, landed at the Berhama airport and strolled to customs to sign the papers for the shipment of onion bulbs that had already been picked up.

"Hello, Graham," Walker Tandem said. Tandem had been the first black Berhamian customs officer—a distinction accountable for many stories in the *Times*. Now he was the oldest. He knew every importer and exporter, every product.

"They got the bulbs all right, Walker?"

"Yes, they did, and they were happy they weren't as heavy as that load of Volclay you had brought in last month. How does that stuff work, anyway?"

Graham set down his bag. The grenades had been smuggled in inside some of the fifty-pound bags. "Well, the best thing is to drain the area first. You know that little pond I have out there; didn't take long. The Volclay comes in pellets, and you mix it in with the mud or dirt at the bottom of the area. Each little pellet of powder swells up to eighty times its original size and it plugs up the earth. Then the earth silts over, you know, and packs the Volclay down some more. That's how the seepage stops. I hope it works the way they say it will. The Dutch use it in their dikes. If it works and we get enough rain, I'll be in good shape. I'll let you know so you can come out and have a look for yourself. Come anyway and get some tomatoes; they're good this year and you know DeSilva's selling them for seventy-five cents apiece."

"Sure will. My best to your folks."

Rattery stuck his receipt in his pocket and went to his pick-up truck. He paused a moment before starting up. Next week, he thought, the old Berhama would be gone. Troops might be sent from England, but the old order would have passed, and the rich from all over the world, now racing down in their yachts and sloops, those who survived and their relatives, would know that terrorism had reached halfway around the world to their private little 31-square-mile playground.

Once settled in the small cottage, Rattery took a quick turn around the farm and gave gifts to his helpers, Clarence, Clifford and Claretson: copies of *Les damnes de la terre*. They shook hands solemnly and they assured him that they had been signed on as waiters for the Royal Berhamian Hotel Providence–Berhama Yacht Race party.

"Looks good," Rattery said. "I can always depend on you."

119

Late in the afternoon, after the three young men had tidied up and put on their black, green and red helmets and driven away on their mopeds, Rattery went to the storehouse where Frithe had placed the onion bulbs andremoved the package of cocaine. He hefted it in his hand. Of the $50,000 he expected to receive from Lapidus, he would keep ten; the rest he would hand over to Frithe. Like foot soldiers, Clarence, Clifford and Claretson knew nothing about the money. At their ages, Rattery thought, and with their knowledge of things, causes were more important. Peter Frithe was once like them, but that had changed. He was now a casualty and was better off to the rear of things.

"Find everything all right?" Frithe asked when Rattery had called him. Frithe was still fighting a hangover.

"Everything's all right. But do you suppose we could talk tomorrow? I'd just like to refresh things."

"Sure," Frithe said. Maybe Rattery would give him the money tomorrow.

"Nothing new politically then?" Rattery said.

"Nothing. See you tomorrow."

Rattery was just about to hang up when Frithe spoke again. "Graham, listen—"

"Yeah?"

"You're sure?"

Rattery paused a moment before answering. Why was Peter asking him now? Was he about to back out? Did he think that he, Rattery, was going to back out? "I wonder at the timing of your question, Peter. Is anything wrong?"

Frithe laughed. "No, man. Nothing's wrong. Like you wanted to refresh things? Well, *I* wanted to refresh things."

"The money's all set, if that's what's worrying you."

"It's not the money. It was never the money, I don't think. I'll see you tomorrow, then, about noon."

Most people saw straight ahead in a perspective that was unvaried right down to the vanishing point; Peter Frithe had always been able to see around the curves, like some of those old Berhamians in the low hills who were said to be experts in witchcraft. Not now, Peter, he thought. Rattery found his hand shaking as he picked up the phone again.

"It's Graham, Sandy." Rattery waited.

"Hi, fella. What time is it?"

"Three. In the afternoon. Everything okay?"

"Yes. Where should I meet you?"

"You still play tennis?"

"Man, you should see my game!"

Rattery laughed. "You mean your backhand's improved?"

"You'll see."

"How about the Ramada Inn tennis courts? At seven tonight."

"You're on. You still using wood?"

"Sure. I suppose you're into graphite?"

"That's the best."

"No, just the most expensive, Sandy. See you then."

By Friday night on Berhama, the high rollers from the Bahamas had flown in, looking for change of scenery and a change of luck. All forms of gambling were illegal on the island, but arrangements were always made and the heavies and light-weights both found the cards and the dice tables.

They played through the weekend, served by trusted island people in the gaming rooms, dining rooms or bedrooms of large cottages. Like gambling, prostitution was illegal on the island; there was none, in fact. For the women were not whores, were not call girls; they were "friends."

Another group, Berhamians, took to the water

Friday evenings, easing out to the coves and reefs and anchoring, then dining and drinking, away from it all. On Saturday mornings they breakfasted and drank Bloody Marys and spent the day alternately swimming and sun bathing. They dressed for dinner Saturday evenings.

Still other Berhamians who did not own boats, clogged the island's roads with their cars as they sought to shop. That done, they headed for their respective clubs, if they were men, or settled down to plan Sunday dinner, if they were women.

And still other Berhamians met at various beaches or homes, built barbeques, played soccer and cricket and drank.

Tourists and other Berhamians stood on line in restaurants all over the island; waiters rushed up and down; bartenders sloshed drinks; muscians talked over the numbers they would play in their first sets; cabs oozed through the streets, well within the thirty-mile-an-hour speed limit. A pair of bobbies, one with fat little legs and chubby buttocks, moved slowly along Dock Street. The great ships at anchor were made more immense by the lights that shone brightly upon them. Occasionally a sports car, engine revving at a traffic light, howled briefly down the street when the light had changed; no sports car on the island had ever even reached 60- of the 120-mile-an-hour capability; the law forbade it, and the traffic laws were harsh.

Rattery stopped to talk to the tennis pro, a thin, rangy man with graying hair. He worked the backboard while waiting for Lapidus. Pleased with his backhand, he began working his forehand, topspin, chips. He had forgotten how pleasant it was to play tennis under the lights instead of in the steaming Berhamian sun. He found it exhilarating and now really looked forward to playing with Lapidus.

Another ball whizzed past him and bounded off the backboard and Rattery stopped and turned. Who else but Lapidus?

"The Big Red," Lapidus said.

Rattery wondered how much Lapidus made these days. At Cornell (Lapidus was in pre-Law) it was assumed that he would do okay, that demonstrating and speaking and raising money for minority movements wouldn't hurt. Rattery never dared challenge his own future for fear he might fail so miserably that he would have to leave Berhama where, in any event, he knew his future lay, one way or the other.

Things hadn't turned out precisely well for either of them. He was a farmer—by choice—but that didn't get you any points. And Lapidus was an agent—or manager—and a dope supplier (once removed). And revolutionaries did not wear $200 tennis shorts. (It never ceased to amaze Rattery that people paid so much for a foot-and-a-half of cloth which, no matter how expensive, still smelled after a match.) That was all over for Sandy Lapidus, the way Boy Scout days were over for men his father's age.

"The Big Red indeed," Rattery said. They touched fingers briefly, each looking deeply into the other's eyes. "I got the rosin," he said, picking up his ball.

Lapidus started to move to the other side of the court. "And I got the bread. Let's play."

Lapidus wondered what Rattery did with money on Berhama. Maybe he was part of some South Atlantic network and only posed as a farmer. But he knew that you didn't ask questions; you just dealt. Still, it was a nagging mystery; Rattery had always given Lapidus the impression that he was forever, irrevocably, a revolutionary, a Bill Kunstler without briefcase. Lapidus settled at the baseline, moved his torso back and forth. I'll do this turkey quick, he thought, finish the deal and get back to Cynthia. Shit. It's Saturday night.

Rattery bent at the knees, wheeled the racket around as he straightened on his toes and caught it perfectly. His forearm vibrated with the hit.

Lapidus stopped moving and looked for the yellow Saxon hardcourt; it was screaming at him, its flight made more soundless by Rattery's grunt. Lapidus gained his poistion, got his racket up and moved in on the ball which tore the racket out of his hand. Startled, Lapidus looked at Rattery. Rattery laughed and called out the score.

"Wednesday night, Norma, Wednesday night."

"I hear you, but I don't believe it, Cynthia." She looked helplessly at her husband.

Mr. Manley snapped his paper. He had known it would come to this. That rotten business about the Miss Berhama contest. Thought she'd gotten over it when she settled down with that Sinclair Archibald boy. Nice enough fellow. Least he wasn't no Rastafarian, and that was half the battle on Berhama. Disgrace. Don't care if he didn't come home one night. "I told you," he said to his wife, snapping his paper again. "I told you."

"Aw, Daddy. I really have to get out of here and this is my chance. I'll send for David within a month, I'm sure."

Mrs. Manley moved a couple of steps and became motionless again. Is this, she wondered, what happened to your children when you worked to make something out of them. No better than a . . . Mrs. Manley couldn't think it. No, not her child.

"And Sinclair? Why *won't* you listen to him, Cynthia? Don't mess up your life like this. Please listen to us."

"She won't listen, can't you see?" Mr. Manley said. He turned a page in the paper, *The Berhama Times*, which he'd already read from front to back four times since picking it up in the morning. He eyed the suitcase and clothes. "Young people, Mother, just don't have the sense we had. We managed in Berhama; the system didn't hurt us at all. Lot's of opportunities and we turned them over to her, and now look."

"Daddy, there never was and never will be nothing for folks like us on this island." Cynthia stopped moving for a moment. "What's there to *do? Where's* there to *go?* How many bands here can afford to pay even what little I'd ask, and even if they did I wouldn't want my career to be just *here.*"

Mr. Manley snorted. "We did all right. You had everything you ever wanted."

"Things have changed, Daddy. They really have. When Sinclair didn't come home that night, the light shone in. I could see earth, sun, sky and water. My life dripping out on 31 square acres of rock upon which very nearly everybody was engaged, one way or another, in kissing some tourist's behind in order to make a living."

Mrs. Manley shot a frightened glance at her husband: he was headwaiter at The Scallop.

"Tourism's been good for everybody," he said sharply. "Everybody. If it wasn't for the tourists we would be walking barefoot and eating grass. Now shut the hell up, Cynthia. And yes, how can you take care of a child doing whatever you plan to do in New York?" He hit the paper with the side of his hand; it snapped double; he smoothed it. "Go on welfare?" he sneered.

"No—"

"Oh, that man's going to get you divorced and marry you and adopt David and you'll live happy forever?"

"Daddy . . ." Cynthia felt a shade less sure of herself.

"You'd best plan not to have the boy. I'm sure Sinclair'll have something to say about that, too."

"I'm going," Cynthia said quietly, forcing defiance into her voice.

"The shame," Mrs. Manley said softly. "What'll they say in church?"

NINE

The ships rushed on, the crewmen feeling an unrecognized urgency to violate the Sunday morning with their work. *The Bastogne* capsized. The other boats, sails drumming in the wind, rushed past after receiving assurances that everyone was okay and would be able to right their vessel. *Magellan* split a sail and slowed, its crew bawling and scrambling for the lockers. *Hot Shot, Loverly, Berhamian; Spoilsport, Eagle, Ne'er Do Well; Encounter, Hawk, Scooter; Pastorale, Don't Mess With Me, Via Veneto; Dime Dancer, Slip Shod, Arrow; Arcturus, Poseidon* and *White Arrow* and the rest, plunged on, down the rhumb line. Some skippers, ignoring the surface and weather reports, swung out eastward, trying to find the Gulf Stream currents and ride them to Berhama. Here and there the smaller ships found themselves abreast of the larger ships; they looked like doves feeding with eagles.

"Hey Sooz, it's me, Gary."

Suzanne Kendrick stretched. Beneath her windowshade she saw the sunlight gleaming like a golden bar. "Hi, where are you?"

"New York."

"Oh. I thought maybe you were back."

"Sometime tomorrow. You okay?"

"Sure. For how long?"

"I dunno. Until sometime after the race, I guess, and then we have to spend some time with Trottingham. Look, I am going to see you?"

"Yes, of course. I thought we had a date."

"Yeah, yeah. That's fine, kid. Can I bring you anything?"

"No. You'll be at the Queen?"

"Where else? Mike and Kevin will be with me."

"Good, I'd like to see them."

"I'm looking forward to seeing you, babes. I'll call you."

Suzanne felt a rush of relief when she hung up. There would be something to do for a couple of days this week at least. She had run out of things to do, places to go. After the round of restaurants, usually for lunch, for she did not like to have dinner out alone, and after the beaches and the various lounges, visited in late afternoon, there was nothing for a person alone to do. She had also taken all the boat trips around the island to the reefs, to St. Gregory's, and mopeded from one disappointing museum to the other. She analyzed her restlessness. Was she ready to return to the mainland? Had she recovered? Did the dissatisfaction with the island indicate that she was no longer dissatisfied with herself? She knew one thing now, and it was that she could not stay on Berhama forever. She had to get back to the agency.

People watching in Berhama had given her some new ideas, models needed to become more universal, somewhat meatier, perhaps not quite as tall and a little less striking. The world was an average place and most of the people in it were average. That needed some reflection. Models needed to become more universal. Maybe, she thought, it took the loss of the boobs to make it hit home. Careful though, Kendrick. Your problem isn't everyone's and people may want to continue to dream.

The cab pulled away from the cottage where Lapidus had spent the night with Cynthia Manley Archibald. He was hungover and she was still asleep trying to get over hers. They drink too much in this place, he thought. If I had to drink as much and the way they do, my ulcer would kill me in a day. They peeled away from the beach onto a hard road leading into Wellington. Lapidus glanced once in the mirror and saw that the driver was studying him. Maybe he knew. It had not made much sense to be renting rooms and cottages until Cynthia told him about her husband and how there were few secrets on Berhama. When walking through the corridors of the Queen, passing the help, Lapidus repressed a desire to turn and see if they were staring at him. Good thing the man, her husband, was not violent, he thought. Or rich enough to hire someone to kick his ass.

At two o'clock he'd be safe when Jax arrived with his entourage, including two bodyguards. Then things would be cool. Lapidus kept his hand on his tennis bag; he didn't want to leave that with its neat little package in the cab. He was glad the deal was settled. Now there was only Cynthia. How could he have thought she had the talent to make it? Maybe that only proved how far and fast he had come in two years. Good-looking, yes. Talented, yes. For Berhama, not for the world. And she was so eager to get away.

She was taking everything all too seriously. (Lapidus had never learned how to handle the dreamers.) Maybe that had to do with how desperate she was to get away. She was going to be difficult, damn it.

But, if he had learned one thing well, it was that beautiful but talentless (compared to New York, Vegas, West Coast talent) women were a dime a dozen in his business.

The cab drivers waiting for fares at the Queen seemed to stare at him when he got out. His own cab driver exhibited a marked coolness in contrast to others he'd had. Lapidus gripped the tennis bag and walked quickly into the hotel. He did not take the elevator until he saw other guests in it—something he'd learned in New York. On his floor he all but sprinted to his rooms, but pulled up short when he saw the slight, youngish woman sitting on the floor in front of his door.

She spoke first. "Are you Mr. Lapidus?" It came out LAPidus.

God, Lapidus thought. Someone who's heard about Jax. A Groupie.

"I'm Linda Churchill," the woman said. "I'm with the *Berhama Times*; do you know it?" She held out her hand, filled with rings, which Lapidus took while glancing over his shoulder down the hall and inserting the key into the lock with the other. "Good to meet you," he said. "You folks go to work early." He opened the door and squeezed in and pushed it back against her.

Churchill, displaying a certain disarming inno-
cence, said, "My friend who's in the suite over
there said you were Jax Bendersen's agent, right?"

"Yes, yes, but I must—"

"She's from NBC news and—"

Lapidus stopped pushing against the door. "NBC?
What's her name?"

"Cromwell. Fern Cromwell."

Mouth agape, eyes wide, Churchill stood waiting, watching the expressions run one after the
other on his face. Not news for Fern, she knew,
but for Siggonson. So she would use NBC as an
entree, just as Fern had suggested. Everybody did
stars, but few writers did the people behind the
scenes. She eased forward.

"Ah, come in, Miss."

"Churchill. Linda Churchill."

Churchill slipped through the door, mouth still
wide, eyes filled with the splendor of the innocent.
"She had to go to St. Gregory's this morning, but
she'll be back to talk to you soon. In the meantime,
I thought you might give an exclusive interview
with my paper."

Jax would be pleased to be on NBC, Lapidus
knew. If this woman had a connection with Cromwell, so be it. Who gave a damn about *The Berhama*

Times? He would do it, and then sit back and wait for the *real* publicity, through television.

"Listen, Linda," Lapidus laughed. "I've had kind of a night, and I'd like to take a shower. Help yourself to a drink or call down for coffee, okay? I'll be out in a couple of seconds."

Churchill watched him walk away with the tennis bag. "Playing tennis all night, Mr. Lapidus?"

"No. That's where the night started." He came back and stood glancing at her. "Would you like to join me in the shower, uh—"

Linda smiled. "Another time, perhaps, thanks. Not now."

Lapidus retreated to the bathroom again. "Okay."

Churchill called for a large pot of coffee, thinking that Mr. LAPidus could use some too, especially if he had been out all night with Cynthia Manley Archibald. Of course, Sinclair did not let any grass grow under his feet either. But that was the way on Berhama—everything at flashpoint—sex, drink and politics. Churchill knew that Siggonson would arch his patchy brows when she handed in the story on *LAPidus—The Man Behind Bendersen.* He would call it featherweight. Then she would give him the other story: the Mandarino business.

Perhaps it might be potent enough—given the support MacKenzie, DeSilva and Donnelly had amassed on both sides of the House—to shake things up and force Trottingham to call for a vote of confidence, which he might very well lose. Then the choice would be Donnelly or DeSilva. Not really a choice at all for the people. Damn it, she thought. Wasn't there anyone else *but* Trottingham?

The racial makeup of the island dictated that Roi Donnelly be Trottingham's successor, with DeSilva becoming his stand-in, his deputy. This information had not been gained in a straightforward on-the-record manner. Churchill had worked at it as with a puzzle, getting some needed aid from Cromwell Friday night. Kneesey meetings with Mac-Kenzie, feelsies drinks here and there and giving it up. Goddamn if she was returning to England. Now it was all on the verge of paying off. Mac-Kenzie had offered to back her with the money needed to start another paper, should the coup come off. And Mandarino and his associates were due down tomorrow—hopefully with a copy of their poll. By the end of this very week, if all went even half-way well, she would never again have to worry about her status as a Berhamian.

The station manager obviously was flattered. Here he lived out his life in a mildewed, termite-ridden nineteenth century house that passed for a studio, using equipment a dozen years old, for the most part. His hands were all part-timers, scrambling at one thing or another until their schedules summoned them to the studio where they more or less put together their shows or manned their machines. The station manager knew that he would never be called to New York, Washington, Chicago or Los Angeles or San Francisco; Berhama produced almost no news. Even the riots were of minor interest to the news chiefs. Berhama produced little advertising revenue for the network. The products advertised were, for the most part, local. It had been his decision to keep in the trailers for products sold only on the mainland to attract accounts from businessmen who might *think* competition was arriving from America.

Of course, he had watched Cromwell deliver the news in her crisp, rhythmic style, the dome of the Senate Building behind her. He was flattered that she had called and invited him to brunch this Sunday morning. Flattered, yes, but cautious also. If she had found a story, he wanted in.

Cromwell sensed his desperation. She also saw it in his crumpled, out-of-style suit, and the way his eyes seemed to linger longest on the most expensive items in the middle of the page on the menu. She finished her Bloody Mary and ordered another round without asking the station manager if he cared for one more. But he smiled when it came. "Down for a little color with the race, I guess," he said.

"Change of pace," Cromwell answered.

"They'll put it in Sports."

"Not the way I want to do it."

"Thirty seconds, that's how much time they'll give you."

Cromwell shrugged. "I'm hoping for a minute fifteen, the way I plan to do it with your help, of course."

The waiter hovered near their table. The station manager looked anxiously at him. "Shall we order?" Cromwell asked.

"If you're ready."

Cromwell leaned forward and gave the station manager her order. That pleased him. He sat back and gave it to the waiter, then gave his; it was the New York steak and eggs. The station manager moved his silver about. "Expensive. We'd have to rent a boat, of course—"

"But wouldn't the Ministry of Tourism supply one?" Cromwell smiled innocently. She thought, the bastard's probably got a relative who rents boats.

"Maybe. If there are any places left. It's kind of late, you know."

"I think they'd be able to find space for NBC, don't you? Will you look into it? I mean, I don't want to trample on your turf. And you do know something about the races, the boats and the people who sail them." She smiled broadly, leaned over the table. "In fact, I hear you once had a boat yourself."

The station manager smiled himself, now, a little weakly. "Yes, I know a little something about the races."

Cromwell leaned back. She took another sip from her drink. "Does the Prime Minister welcome the winners?"

"Trottingham? Certainly not," the station manager spluttered.

"I thought he gave away trophies or something."

"No."

"He'll be there, though."

"At some of the functions. Some he'll hold at his house."

"He's not a very popular man, is he? I mean I get the impression that—"

"He's Dock Street's man at the moment. And they don't care about the people."

"In the unlikely event that a change became necessary, who would replace him?"

The station manager, seeing something lurking behind Cromwell's words, became cautious. "What do you mean?"

"Who would make a good Prime Minister in Trottingham's absence?"

139

The station manager nodded. "I see. Well." He stroked his neck with his index finger. "There are a number of people who'd like to be Prime Minister—"

"Who would be *most* likely?"

The station manager needed more from Cromwell than just breakfast. He laughed as the meal came. "Now, Miss Cromwell, I just don't know."

"It would be Donnelly or DeSilva, wouldn't it?" she asked quickly and harshly, as though she had run out of patience with him. "Donnelly or DeSilva because Dock Street could control them, isn't that right?" The waiter placed their meals before them.

The station manager chewed his steak without comment. It was the first one he'd had in a couple of weeks and he wished to enjoy it. He swallowed, too hurriedly to enjoy the mouthful, because he wanted to say: "Even Dock Street might be wrong about who it can control."

Cromwell had been an only child and had no older brothers or sisters to defend her. She had learned to attack and attack and study her opponents' eyes. "Something happens in the eyes," her father told her, teaching her the old one-two. "You watch the eyes; that's what good boxers do. The eyes."

The station manager was stung. Cromwell attacked with scorn.

"Hell, down here black people don't seem to mind being controlled by any Tom, Dick or Harry. At least Dock Street throws them crumbs because it needs their vote." She laughed. "Are you trying to tell me that Dock Street *doesn't* control this place and the people?" She finished her drink and ordered another round. The station manager raised his hand too late in protest. "Do you know something other people don't? I mean, I'm not surprised. They told me you were a pretty good newsman. Everything's in the bag, isn't it, and Mandarino's just frosting on the cake."

The station manager grimaced; she had advanced too far and too fast. She was fishing now. Chewing calmly now, even royally, taking delicate little swallows, he studied her, wondered how many people she'd been to bed with to make it to the top. That's the way the world still was. He himself had broken in a countless number of young things interested in getting into television, including that Cynthia Manley Archibald. You want to do a little song and dance on the talent hour? You want to be a script girl? You want to do the weather for us? You want to be a reporter? Why sure, young lady, this way. Er, there, over on the couch.

"Every one who looks the fool, is not the fool, Miss Cromwell. And every one who acts the fool, is not the fool."

"There are two major fools, I'm told," Cromwell said.

"Is that so?" The station manager smiled. "The island is filled with fools, and they all think they are major—or important."

"Hey, look Freddie, let's stop the bullshit."

The station manager stopped chewing and surveyed the distance between them. "I beg your pardon."

"That nigger with the chickens and that spic with the supermarkets, what are they up to? Just who are they supposed to double-cross?"

Outerbridge was wearing a large straw hat against the blinding sun. His sunglasses kept slipping down along the bridge of his nose. He looked gratefully at his motionless line dangling over the side of the boat; he was hoping he would not get a bite because he hated to handle fish. His companion would have to land it and unhook it, just as he had baited the line for Outerbridge in the first place.

Vernon Summerall, also in dark glasses, and wearing a long-billed cap that further shaded his face, felt more secure on the water than in any office, street, restaurant or other meeting place on the island. Super-security. Where else would fishermen and boat people be on a fine Sunday morning? It was natural that they were there. Week days, not so good, even if they'd had the time.

142

"I know it's crazy," Summerall said. He opened a can of Coke and sipped from it. "But, that's the way things go sometimes. A lot of things happening all at once, some related, some not. We don't want to chase the decoy back and find that they've gone right down the middle and scored. Know what I mean?"

Outerbridge said, "I think so. Your American football is hard to understand. I wish you knew something about soccer or cricket."

"It doesn't matter. We just want to be assured that Berhama is going to stay essentially the way it is. That's important to us."

"I understand that," Outerbridge said breezily. "You don't want to be surrounded by hostile or at least unresponsive entities. I know all that."

"I know you do." He drank in silence, and after a time Summerall said, "Trottingham troubles us. He behaves like the place was his private fiefdom. Didn't they know what that fellow was really like when they booted out Basil Siggonson?"

"He made all the right sounds," Outerbridge said. "They believed him because they wanted to, and they thought they could control him."

"The crunch will be whether or not he takes Frithe onto his board. If he doesn't, as we have suggested through some of our friends, they will coup his ass and that might not be a bad idea."

"I don't know if Frithe would do it."

"I know. But if he won't, that will tell us something important."

"Change in tactics," Outerbridge said.

Summerall took off his hat and wiped his forehead and replaced it. "We think we understand Frithe and what he wants for the people. If he takes it, people aren't going to think for too long that he's sold out; they'll believe he got wise. The workers who dumped him will approve of him; the middle class will like him because he's reformed and the whites will okay him."

"Because they okay every black man who's willing to come inside the system instead of staying outside of it where they might do harm."

Summerall smiled at his companion. "Oh!" he said. "Why doesn't Mrs. Trottingham like you?"

Outerbridge laughed. "Her gardener. She had an affair with her gardener. She knows I know."

Summerall laughed softly. "Old Greta. Would you believe it?" He started the engine. "Let's move. Nothing here." They pulled up the anchor and moved to another spot a mile away. Summerall glanced at the lines. "Nothing on the troll, eh? Looks like a bad day." He finished his Coke and lit a pipe. "If Trottingham doesn't want Frithe, then MacKenzie and the rest'll push hard for Donnelly or DeSilva—probably harder for Donnelly. That would put a better uh, complexion on things." He smiled at Outerbridge who, with his hat pulled down, his arms folded across his chest, seemed to be dozing. But he laughed softly and then yawned. They both knew that Donnelly would nationalize faster than the Opposition would, if it had the chance. And they knew that MacKenzie and the rest of The Dock Street Gang didn't know it. "He's clever that one," Summerall said.

"Aw, he just wants to do what Trottingham's doing. Be the boss."

"Yes, but while he's being the big boss what happens to our interests here, and who says that he and his chickens are above persuasion by some foreign entities? No. Trottingham's the man for now and—"

"—then Frithe."

"Right, my friend. He's the man of the near future. You can count on ex-revolutionaries to behave."

Outerbridge started to laugh, softly and slowly at first and then louder and louder; he turned onto his side on the deck and howled. Watching him, Summerall grinned. "Hey, what's so funny?"

"You know," Outerbridge gasped. "Frithe—Frithe and Rattery—"

"The hand grenades!" Now Summerall laughed. "I—I can't wait."

When their laughter had spent itself, Summerall checked the lines with disgust. "I don't know where the fish are today. Let's move again." They hoisted the anchor and moved further out to sea.

Now Outerbridge pulled a can of beer from the ice. "You know that Mandarino is contributing more to his country than he'll ever realize by helping to keep Trottingham in office. Now if only the Prime Minister will see beyond his pettiness to Frithe. . . ."

And Frithe, Summerall thought, still grinning with Outerbridge, is just the man we want, for he is bereft of the killer instinct. He *loves* people, even if they wind up not loving him. He wants to improve their lot, raise them to higher levels, teach them goodness. God, how we can work with him!

TEN

"I've never seen this place so busy," Mandarino said.

They walked quickly across the torrid runway, hurrying to get through customs.

"It's the boat race," Mike Brooks said.

"Should be a lotta women around," Kevin Levy said.

Mandarino shook his head. Women. That was about all Levy ever thought about. He glanced over his shoulder. The other passengers were rushing behind them like a multi-colored tidal wave. "Hurry up," he said, and increased his speed.

"How long will you be here?" the customs officer asked Mandarino.

"Three days."

"On business, Sir?"

"Yes."

The officer passed Mandarino a card. Mandarino groaned. "Will you please read that?"

"I've read it before."

"Good. Open your bag, please."

Mandarino glanced at Brooks and Levy who'd gone through without trouble and were waiting for him. "Shit," Mandarino said.

He opened his bag and glared at the officer as he felt, patted, skimmed his fingers around inside it, and then repeated his movements. He seemed to sigh as he said, "All right, Sir. You can close it. Thank you."

Mandarino snatched his bag. "I want that son-ofabitch fired."

"Is he the one you draw all the time?" Brooks asked.

"No." Mandarino led the way to the taxi stand. "They all do it to me."

"You want them all fired?" Levy said.

"Yeah, every fuckin' one of them."

Brooks and Levy laughed. "You," Mandarino said to Brooks. "They act like you're more American than me."

"I am," Brooks said. "We didn't come there via no pizza boat, you know."

"What the fuck you laughin' at, Kevin? They didn't even *let* Jews on this goddamn rock until twenty years ago."

In the cab Brooks said, "We'll get the Minister for Home Affairs to get us some papers, Gary, so we don't have to go through that shit. That's Donnelly."

"Great. But why didn't you do that before? Jesus. People lookin' at me, and that creep—he was disappointed that he didn't find anything."

"Once," Levy said, "I took this flight to Cairo—"

"Once I got my ass kicked on the border between Mississippi and Alabama," Brooks said, "And—"

"All right, all right," Mandarino said. He was silent a moment, watching the countryside, the people walking along the roads, the pastel-colored houses, the brief vistas of the blue-green sea. He started to laugh.

"Yeah?" Levy said.

"I think I'll put a snake in my bag the next time."

Brooks laughed. "It'd better be poison."

"Who's got that tick-list handy?" Mandarino held out his hand for it. Receiving it from Levy, he studied it and handed it back.

"Okay," he said. "We'll talk about it at the hotel."

They did not talk about their work in cabs. The drivers were repositories for information and nearly all of them were members of the Opposition.

Cost of living, Mandarino was thinking. Wage controls, but no price controls? Not cool, Trotts, not cool at all. And what else was on that list? Yeah, Mike's Rhodesia package. Servants to the world? What could they really do about that? Not much. Play with words. Suggest light industry—assembling Japanese goods, perhaps, since they were becoming incredibly expensive. But you couldn't get these people to work for Japanese wages. Brooks was right, though. *So many slaves so many foes.* That was Roman—or Italian, whatever.

Not our concern, he thought, but . . . Mandarino wrote on a piece of paper and passed it to Levy. The writing said: Poll stats?

Levy nodded.

They could, Mandarino thought, lay out the real figures for Trottingham. Maybe they would scare him into doing precisely what they advised. That often worked.

Trottingham was not the first balky client they'd ever handled; not the first to go swinging wildly on his own without consulting them. Such clients, if they lost their elections, of course blamed their defeats on mishandling by Mandarino Associates. And you couldn't have a string of defeated clients in this business, he thought. Our reputation is on the line. And Trottingham and his Dock Street Gang were not going to screw that up.

Phipps met them at the desk as they were checking in. "Are we confirmed for the meetings tonight, gentlemen?"

They turned to greet him and to be told of any untoward events that might have occurred. There were none, Phipps told them; just the usual intra-party squabbles, the well-timed Monday morning blast by Ida Jones-Williams in Siggonson's paper.

"Mr. MacKenzie is the host tonight," Phipps said. "Cabinet members will be there, including the Prime Minister."

"We will want to see Trottingham alone afterward," Mandarino said.

"I'll tell him and get back to you," Phipps said. "I don't think he has any plans for later except to return home."

"Good. It's important."

"Rest well," Phipps said. He strode off through the lobby of the Queen looking like one of those legendary British Army sergeants in civilian dress.

Mandarino, Levy and Brooks took their keys and started for the elevator. The man who'd registered them retreated to a corner of the desk and picked up a phone.

Sinclair Archibald said to Fern Cromwell, "Mandarino is in 520, Brooks in 522, and Levy in 524."

"Ah, thank you, darling. See you tonight?"

"Yes." And they have a meeting tonight at MacKenzie's."

"I'll want you to do something for me, if you can—"

"We'll see, Fern. I've got to go."

Cromwell called *The Berhama Times* and was put through a series of people until, at last, Linda Churchill answered. "They're here and I've got the room numbers."

"Fantastic," Churchill said.

"They're meeting at MacKenzie's tonight."

"What time?"

"Listen, honey, I don't know. How much work do you expect me to do for you? Stake out the damned place." Cromwell breathed in exasperation. The girl had done an interview with her, with Bendersen's agent, and she, Cromwell, would arrange to get a copy of the poll stats for both of them to look at, and Churchill was still asking questions.

Unruffled Churchill asked, "Is the project still on then, while they're out tonight?"

"I'll take care of the key. You get the photographer for meeting."

"All right. I'll handle the meet. Check with you later."

"I've got two meetings tonight" Mandarino was saying into the phone. "But maybe we can gather for a late dinner or something, okay?"

"Great," Suzanne Kendrick said. "Do you want me to meet you somewhere?"

"Well, Sooz, I don't know when I'll be through or where I'll be. Let me call you and then we can meet somewhere."

"Fine with me, babes," she said.

The knocking on Mandarino's door became more insistent. "Okay, okay," he said. He went to the door and opened it to admit Brooks and Levy who were dressed for the pool. Mandarino stripped and pulled on his trunks. "I've been thinking about that tick-list, you guys. It wouldn't look good if the

153

Government suddenly rescinded those laws from Rhodesia." Mandarino glanced at Brooks. "Call attention to them. Maybe we can get the Prime Cut not to pass them to the other House, know what I mean? Just let 'em lay where they are."

"Okay," Levy said.

"What about those poll stats?" Brooks asked.

"Yeah. I think we'd better let him have them right between the eyes. That's why we want to see him after the tap dance."

"Is that wise, Gary?"

"Tell ya, Kevin. We gotta jerk that cocksucker up short. We can't threaten him. It's not our country, just our client. So we lay it on him. If he's gonna catch up with DeSilva and Donnelly, he's gotta be a big boy and not ignore our advice."

Levy snorted. "More fuckin' trouble with his own people than with the Opposition."

"We'll just drop the shit on him, that's all," Mandarino said.

They started out of the room. Mandarino stopped. "Who's got the stats?"

"Me," Brooks said.

"Locked?"

"Yeah."

"Shit's delicate, you know."

Brooks and Levy looked at each other. They smiled.

Downstairs the Settlers' Bar was packed. The lobby was filled. All of a type, Mandarino thought. Sun-bleached hair, deep tans, smelling of perfumes and sun-tan oil. Boat people.

They picked up some drinks and drifted to the pool and stretched out on the chaises. All wore dark glasses.

"Hey, hey, hey," Levy said.

"Where?" Brooks said.

"Over there. Near the entrance to the restaurant. Ain't she somethin'?"

"I don't see," Mandarino said.

"With the lime-colored suit on."

"Oh. Yeah, yeah. Jesus. Look at the legs on her will you?"

"Oh, oh," Brooks said.

"Where?" Levy strained up out of his seat. "Oh, the one coming this way." He sat back down and groaned.

"Nice day," Mandarino said to the woman. She smiled and walked on past.

"I could go crazy here," Levy said. "I could fall in love."

"Hey, Mike, make arrangements to get this fucker laid somewhere, huh?"

Brooks said, "Shit. Every man for himself."

Mandarino smiled. Okay. I got my date for tonight. Suzanne. He said, "I don't know how I got tied up with a couple of turkeys like you two. Don't you know from cool yet?"

"Let's do a disco tonight," Levy said.

"Yeah, Gary. When we finish with these people we're going to need some heavy R & R."

"Yeah, maybe." He closed his eyes and forced himself to relax. It would be good to be with Suzanne again. "Lemme alone," Mandarino said. "I want to sleep."

"Now," Brooks said, "that's cool."

Mandarino rested, enjoying the sounds of voices, the splashes in the pool, the hot sun on his flesh. He never seemed to realize how tired he was until he got a chance to rest. Brooks' voice came to him.

"Gary, you gotta see this. Who is that guy, Kevin?"

"Jax Bendersen. God, look at the broads he's got with him."

Bendersen, Mandarino saw, moved slowly down the opposite side of the pool. He was tall and blond, wore his hair long and had a neat beard. He seemed

tired, or perhaps drunk. Behind him came two big
men, both wearing sunglasses, whose heads kept
swiveling; behind them walked an assortment of
people, men and women, all in swim suits, all talking loudly, frantically.

"They're high," Brooks announced.

"Yeah? How can you tell?" Mandarino wanted
to know.

"Watch them. I wonder—they're tough on dope
in this place. Do we have a Berhama Connection
or something?"

"Aw, you're fulla shit," Mandarino said, closing
his eyes again. "The girls are nice, though. Goddamn nice."

Levy and Brooks watched one of the laughing
girls walk into a steel lightpost near the pool. Still
laughing, she ricocheted back and to the side,
rubbed her forehead with a puzzled expression and
continued on, laughing.

"Jesus," Levy said.

"You know," Mandarino was saying as they
walked up the driveway to MacKenzie's house,
"I think we're going to have to lay it out for these
people. Tonight. We'll get it straight or tell them
we walk. Kevin, what do you think?"

"Okay."

"Mike?"

"Okay."

"You got the stats?"

"No. I left them. I didn't think we ought to show a red flag to the bulls. We can pick it up later to show Trotts."

"Yeah, okay."

"I suppose they call this a cottage, too," Levy said. "You could put twenty Catskill cottages in this baby."

"Listen," Mandarino said almost whispering, for they were at the door now, "all these guys have dough. They are just loaded—more loaded than they have to be for us. Did you see the latest Dun & Bradstreet?"

The door opened and Mandarino said to the middle-aged woman in black serving dress and white apron, "Mandarino Associates."

"Please come in, Sir."

Mandarino saw Brooks give the lady an extra length of nod. He always seemed to do that with other black people. Acknowledging the bond between them?

"Just walk straight through and out into the garden," the woman said, smiling briefly at Brooks.

In the garden they shook hands with the cabinet

members and with the members of The Dock Street Gang. They smiled and joked; they drank and ate from the foods that came without end. They told stories; they listened to stories as they moved back and forth across the lawn.

"Can we gather somewhere, Kirkland," Mandarino said, "so I can do some talking? I mean that's a part of why we're here, right?"

"Yes, yes. Of course." Trottingham walked off to round up the people. Mandarino chatted with Donnelly. Everyone secured refills, as though preparing for passage through a desert. Levy and Brooks pulled up a table and laid their cases against its legs.

Trottingham said, "I think you can go ahead now, Gary. And you will want to field some questions."

"Okay," Mandarino said, and then to the assorted group, "Hello, again. Seems like I just did this a few days ago with some of you, but that's what we get paid for." He smiled. "That and producing victories. But, I have to talk rather seriously with you tonight about the state of the campaign. First, I want to say that we took the account because we believed you were sincere when you told us that Berhama must be integrated. I believe in integration. *We* believe in integration. Furthermore, while some people elsewhere believe that they cannot afford integration financially, we know that you can. In the final analysis, however, in a place such as Berhama, you will not survive with*out* integration.

"We—Mandarino Associates—are in a fortunate position. We don't take just any account. We don't need to. And we never have. We accept accounts, we accept clients, because we believe in what they want to do—if we feel that what they want to do is in the best interests of humanity. Strange to hear a public relations man say that? Well, we are unusual. And that's precisely why everyone wants us.

"Hear, hear!" came from the back of the group.

"I want to make sure that you understand our philosophy and our position because what I'm going to say next may make you unhappy for a while."

Brooks looked out at the faces, some of them folding slowly with the drink, and thought of the South African *Broerderbond*. The four black faces didn't count.

Levy watched the faces and thought of the swastika as the Nazis had used it.

Mandarino continued: "From time to time we are cautioned that it must not appear as though we, Mandarino Associates, are dictating to your government."

Trottingham winced. This was something he had said to Mandarino many times.

160

"I want to assure you categorically that we are not here to run your government. With all of you able gentlemen? No way. You hired us to perform a service for you and that is precisely what we are trying to do.

"*Trying* to do? Gentlemen." Mandarino opened his arms. "We are not your enemies, but often you treat us as though we were. Otherwise, where are the programs each of you ministers was to provide for us? Otherwise, why do rumours persist that some of *you* are supplying the Opposition with funds, as a form of insurance should this party lose the election?"

Levy passed Mandarino a drink during the staged pause. Mandarino sipped it and began to pace back and forth in the small space in front of the table.

"Yes," he said. "But it's only a rumour. I refuse to believe that where there's smoke there's fire; I've gotta feel the fire." He half-turned to Brooks and Levy and winked. He felt a current moving through the group. "Not rumours, but facts, are the leaks that come out of the Cabinet. But, if you don't mind, why should we? Some of the things we discuss are sensitive and also tactical. If you don't care, let us know tonight and we'll plan the overall strategy to accommodate leakages."

Many hands at this point reached casually into pockets, ostensibly for cigarettes or handkerchiefs and shut off recorders.

"But the overall campaign will suffer tremendously."

"Rhodesia, Gary," Brooks whispered.

Mandarino nodded. "People often find governments to be unreal things they cannot grasp. They tend to let the good that governments may create slip past; they're accepted as the norm; that's what governments are for. Our experience tells us that, and we pass it on to you freely. But the bad that governments do, sooner more than later, springs into prominence.

"I refer now to what our colleague calls, The Rhodesia Package." Mandarino smiled at the cautious grunts. "Rhodesia. You members of Parliament are thinking of laws that we would consider to be oppressive, if exercised."

Trottingham stood waving his hand, a punctuation mark in the hubbub. "Gary, could you be more specific?" His tone challenged.

Mandarino smiled benevolently. "The Opposition slumbers—to your advantage. In almost any country in the world today—any country—should a government attempt to pass legislation such as—"

Mandarino gathered himself, remembering, "—a curfew, increasing the police force if there has been no notable increase in crime, increasing the size of the armed forces—that is, the army—when you have no enemies, and permitting certain groups to have target practice; that government would be run out of office. Yet, you are in Parliament discussing such laws. Berhamians are not the Germans of the early 1930's, not the Poles of the late 1920's, not the Spanish under Franco. The Opposition does sleep. And you are lucky it does."

Mandarino took another sip of his drink. He wondered what time it was getting to be.

"All this may seem to some of you that we are trying to run your government. Ah, no. We are trying to help you maintain a nation that already possesses a representative government. You all know the alternatives; you speak of being without the luxury of time. I think you're right. Therefore, the advice we offer you—and it is, after all, advice because you are responsible men and understand consequences—is only that. When we, with our experience in political affairs, perceive that a client has taken the wrong turn, we don't feel that we can continue to take his money if we tell him he's taking the wrong turn and he insists on taking it. At that point we suggest that the client go home and think over the relationship we have with him."

Mandarino finished his drink and passed it behind him to Brooks. "Finally, there's this. A political party that's in disarray will win nothing but the leavings, never the prize. The Berhama United Party, as we see it, has more fights within it than with the Opposition. You have a party leader; he is the man, the boss. You chose him, now you

163

should support him. Politically, that's the only thing you can do.

"And now. We're down to see the finish of the race and to enjoy the celebrations. I hope that you'll give careful consideration to what I said; my colleagues concur. As the Prime Minister suggested, maybe I can handle a few questions—"

Two flashes lighted up the group. Mandarino turned quickly to Brooks and Levy. "Fuckin' photographer out there." He took Brooks' drink and sipped it. MacKenzie's guests were running, staggering and walking confusedly toward the spot behind them where the flashes had come from.

"That bloody goddamn Siggonson," Trottingham was shouting. "That bloody shit Siggonson."

MacKenzie was shouting and stamping his foot. "So, yes, we bought ourselves a public relations agency. Let it come out. Fuck that bloody rag of Siggonson's."

Mandarino noted that DeSilva and Donnelly didn't seem unduly upset.

"Why don't we collect Trottingham and go?" Levy suggested

"Yeah," Mandarino mumbled, glancing at his watch. "Let's get the fuck outa here. Kirkland. Kirkland. Prime Minister!"

"Outerbridge," Trottingham said when they

164

were all seated in his car. The others were still talking amongst themselves in the garden or poking along its outer edges, still looking for the photographer. "Did you see a cameraman lurking about?"

"No, Sir. Nothing." He laughed. "To tell you the truth, Sir, I was dozing."

"All right." He turned to Mandarino. "That was pretty much an ultimatum you delivered tonight, wasn't it? Good. Bloody damned good. Maybe now I can get some cooperation from that Cabinet and the benches."

"There's more," Mandarino said. "That's why we wanted to see you."

Trottingham stared at him as the car moved off toward Wellington.

"More?" he asked. He glanced at Levy and Brooks. He sat back, but pulled away somewhat; he was sitting next to Brooks. Mandarino was on the other side, and Levy was sitting in front with the driver. "Well. To my house then?"

"We have to pick up something at the hotel, first," Brooks said.

"I see. Well, all right. Stop at the Queen, Outerbridge."

They rode in silence until Trottingham said, "In light of what you were saying tonight, perhaps you

165

ought to know that I've decided to take on Peter Frithe as a member of the board of my bank." Deciding that perhaps they didn't know who Frithe was, he continued. "He's a black man. Very active in union organization here—"

"He ran them, didn't he?" Brooks asked quietly, as though he was unsure, but Trottingham knew that at least Brooks knew who Frithe was.

"Yes, I suppose he did," Trottingham said. "Anyway, he had a run of bad luck—"

Brooks was chuckling.

"—and the membership decided that he wasn't the caliber of leader they wanted, so they dropped him. He's not a *bad* chap, and he won't be called on to do much."

"Token, is he?" Mandarino said.

Trottingham stuttered.

"Good move," Mandarino said. "From union organizer to bank director. We can do something with that, Kirkland."

"I'm glad you approve."

"He's popular enough to be in the next poll," Brooks said.

Trottingham started.

Mandarino said soothingly, "That's a good idea,

Kirkland. We do want to keep tabs on all the popular people. It's the wise thing to do."

Trottingham nodded.

ELEVEN

Thirty minutes after Mandarino, Levy and Brooks had left the hotel, Sinclair Archibald called Fern Cromwell.

"Your friends have left."

In her most seductive voice Cromwell said, "Do you suppose you could sneak up here for a few minutes?"

Archibald hesitated. "Just a few?"

"Would I lie?"

As soon as it was convenient, Archibald made

an excuse and sauntered down the hall to the elevator. Out of sight of the desk, his excitement grew. A quickie. The way it used to be with Cromwell. He almost trotted off the car at the tenth floor.

"Sinclair?"

"Uh, yeah," he said, his knuckles still poise against her door. Oh, man, he thought.

Cromwell opened the door quickly. "C'mon in." She closed it just as quickly. Archibald was surprised to see the woman from *The Berhama Times* there.

"Oh, hello, Miss Churchill."

"Mr. Archibald."

Cromwell kissed Archibald. Then her mouth slid up to his ear. "Give Linda your pass key, baby."

Archibald stepped back. Cromwell moved closer. "For ten minutes, Sinclair." She kissed him again and stroked his body.

"I could lose—"

"No you won't. It'll be all right. You owe me, man. Do it."

Archibald handed Churchill the keys and she headed for the door.

"Which one will you start with?" Cromwell asked, already pushing Archibald toward the bed.

169

"Alphabetically, of course."

"Got luggage keys?"

"Of course."

"Even if you get it in five minutes, don't come back for twenty," Cromwell said.

"Right." Churchill moved smoothly around them. "Have fun."

Just as the door closed Cromwell said, "Get those clothes off, Sinclair. We have work to do."

"Oh," Archibald said. Already undressed, Cromwell lay on the bed waiting. What you want, go out and get, her father had taught her. Most times it worked. Like now.

It was strange, Archibald thought, how eager he had been before this moment. Now he felt like a trapped rabbit. "How much longer will you be here, sweetheart?" he asked.

Cromwell enfolded her arms about him, then her legs. "Not much longer, baby, not much longer."

She was, Churchill reflected, better at this sort of thing than she thought she would be. She moved quickly across Brooks' room, the luggage keys already out. If, she thought, if the poll is here, I'm set for life. The possibility that the poll had been carried to the meeting loomed large. But there would certainly be a copy around. And it would be locked up.

The keys jingled lightly in her fingers. She approached the one bag, grateful that this member of Mandarino Associates, at least, travelled lightly. That made her search easier. And faster.

The bag opened with the fourth key.

The blue folder with the cut-out middle read simply:

BERHAMA

Churchill took out a pad and pencil and sat down on the bed with the poll in her lap. Concentrating, she quickly went through the pages, making notes in shorthand: Opinion Poll: Trottingham's behind—She went back to concentrating on the figures, the names beside them. She could savor her surprise later. Issues: Income: White males: Black males: White females: Black females: Age: Voting district: Party affiliation: Favorable: Unfavorable: Don't know:

Every couple of minutes she glanced at her watch. The paper had two photographers out at the meeting. The photos together with this information would make even Siggonson dance an Irish jig. Churchill's pencil flew across the pad; she whipped filled pages back with a crackling sound. But somewhere in her head a question began insisting itself on her consciousness. It was not guilt that she had entered someone's room, opened his bag and was in the process of pilfering political secrets. No. The wrong that men had always done to women gave her extreme satisfaction in what she was doing at the moment.

To be sure, Siggonson had pushed her and other women reporters beyond the brink of journalistic ethics. But how would he play this information? Seventy-two point type, yes, and poison laced from the lead down through the story. The final paragraph was where he usually placed the equivocal information. Would such news be good for Berhama: She knew of no one—even with his multitude of faults—who was better in the office than Trottingham. Petty. Prissy. Two-faced. Ambitious for history to move his family to the top. Like ice, devoid of feeling.

Churchill wrote faster, trying to close off the thoughts now flooding her mind.

Trottingham *was* better than Siggonson's brother, too. Donnelly would be a disaster for Berhama and DeSilva not much better. The front benches held no one with ability, though old Mr. MacKenzie thought otherwise. The back bench, forget it.

She started to feel a cramp from her speed and the tension. She flexed her fingers. Maybe, she thought as she returned to the poll, it was time for her to move on. Compromised in one place, journalists have no other choice but to move on where there is less compromise or where there is none at all, although Linda Churchill could not think where that might be except in a place where there was no paper whatsoever, and therefore no reason to be a journalist.

H.M.S. *Dauntless* moved out of the Wellington Harbor at 2200 hours, headed for St. Gregory's. Communications was already picking up signals from the fleet sailing down from Providence, therefore it was necessary to get into position off St. Gregory's Head to check them in as they crossed the finish line. Already aboard were the officials and more would follow just before dawn. Then, soon after would come the press boats and the motley armada that usually took part in the "Meeting the Yachts" ceremonies.

The night was especially humid. Even the breeze blowing in from the sea through the opened window in Trottingham's study didn't help.

"Kirkland," Mandarino was saying, "we didn't want to get into this in front of the others. It was just as well that we had that interruption. Look, let those Rhodesia laws, as we call them, lay where they are. Don't try to force them through; they can hurt us. Also, on the wage control business, take it from us: either drop it or come up with the companion piece, which has got to be voluntary price controls."

173

Trottingham cleared his throat several times and looked at the drink in his hand.

"The time's just not right," Levy said.

"If the Opposition wakes up," Brooks said, "you can say that you've simply decided not to push those laws through—"

"—after careful consideration," Mandarino added.

"Then if someone asks, 'what careful consideration,' you tell them that you were afraid people would misunderstand the import of the laws," Brooks said. "By the way, Mr. Prime Minister, what did you have in mind?"

"Never mind," Mandarino said. He wanted this business over with tonight so he could get to Suzanne. "Let's go over the polls." Brooks handed him the filefolder with the cut-out middle. "Kirkland, we've got a lot of work to do. You've probably guessed this already, but here it is in black and white; both Donnelly and Desilva pulled many more points than you. In fact, some of the other names we threw into the pot pulled more than you did. We've got to be careful and you've got to follow our advice. I can't say that too often. If you want to win, we can help.

"Now, none of these people have your responsibility, so all of the points they have over you are fluff."

"I see," Trottingham said.

"If the others knew precisely what the point spread was, you'd have a very difficult time with them, as far as we can see," Brooks said.

Levy said, "Yet, we can use their popularity to boost you solidly ahead of them."

Trottingham nodded.

"This Frithe business sounds good, Kirkland," Mandarino said. "There's an obvious and bitter split between the whites and the blacks, and the whites are going to have to take the first step, right Mike?"

"No doubt about it."

"Yes, yes," Trottingham said. "But what do we do about the pictures that were taken tonight? We'll be all over the paper tomorrow."

"I've been thinking about that," Mandarino said. "Maybe it's better now than later. 'Big New York PR firm to help BUP win the election.' I'd hate for that to break in a place like this three or four days before the actual election."

"Look, everyone suspects anyway. Dock Street bringing in the big guns, taking polls, giving advice," Brooks said. "This place needs a little of the twentieth century to blow through it, and maybe our approach should stress the modernization of politics in Berhama."

"Maybe it needs a press conference," Levy said.

"No press conference," Mandarino said. "At least not for us. Can Phipps pull one together if we help him?"

"I don't see why not," Trottingham said. "Yes, a press conference would indeed be helpful. Er, would I have to be there?"

"Would you prefer not to be?" Mandarino asked.

"I certainly wouldn't mind, but shouldn't I keep a certain uh distance?"

"Let DeSilva do it," Brooks said. "Doesn't he have Information?"

"Yes, he does."

Mandarino said, "Great. He'd be announcing our presence in the area of his responsibility. Sort of an announcement that we're taking over from him."

"He never does a gotdamn thing anyway," Trottingham snorted.

"I'll draft a statement that he can read," Brooks said. "I think most of the ministers spend too much time casting slurs on each other for them not to have statements at hand, and questions limited to ten minutes."

"Maybe the lead—'The Prime Minister has asked me to announce'—you know, get Mr. Trottingham's presence in early," Levy said.

176

"When?" Mandarino said.

"Tomorrow would be ideal," Trottingham said, "but the bloody boat race is going to draw everyone's attention."

"I understand that the black people are not involved in the boat race, Mr. Prime Minister."

Trottingham looked through the lights across the room to where Brooks was sitting. He decided that he didn't like him much.

Watching, Mandarino said, "Mike, I think there must be some white people who read the paper, too. Point is, we've got to get on with it, because I know the pictures will be ready tomorrow morning or, at the latest, the day after. They go to bed at ten?"

"Yeah," Levy said, "and it was close to that when those flashes went off."

"They could go a little late," Brooks said, "for a story as big as they think this one is."

"They wouldn't want to rush it," Mandarino said. "They'd want to check with some of the leaks, pull together a lot of stuff they've only been hinting at about our past campaigns." He sighed. "I think the day after tomorrow. But I think we'd better get the statement ready tonight. Just in case." To Trottingham he said, "Did you take all those statistics down, Kirkland? We can get you a full set the next time we're down. We will have had the explosion and the smoke'll be gone then, and if you misplace your folder, it won't be a disaster."

"You will come by tomorrow afternoon for drinks, won't you? There'll be some of the boat crowd, and of course you'll go to the drink-out at the hotel."

"Yes, we'll come if we don't have to gather quickly for an emergency before then. Will you alert Phipps?"

"I'll take care of it, Gary." He stood and stretched. "You'll have some time to yourselves. Enjoy it. Outerbridge will drop you off—anywhere you want to go."

As they were making their way to the garage, Trottingham said, "Do you suppose there's a way you could make them uh, the cabinet members, the party members, er, ah, show a bit more respect for me?"

Mandarino, Levy and Brooks halted. They avoided looking at each other. Mandarino heard the waves slapping against the dock; Levy heard the car engine running; Outerbridge had heard them come up. And Brooks listened to the tree frogs—peepers they called them in the States—and the incessant sounds they were making.

"Like standing up when you enter a room, and not leaving it before you do?" Mandarino said gently.

"Uh, yes. After all, I am the head of state and ah—"

Brooks said, "We noticed that Mr. Trottingham. Part of the party's morale problem. We can work on that. Good idea."

Mandarinio nodded. "No problem, Kirkland. Good night."

In the car they were silent until the driver gained the main road.

"Drop us at the best disco in town," Levy said. "Where the most women are."

Outerbridge laughed. "Women? We have beautiful women everywhere in Berhama."

"Look, you guys. I'm tired. Drop me off at the hotel. And maybe you'd better not disco all night either. Got that statement to do."

"That's not a problem," Levy said. "And we'll be able to sleep late."

Mandarino got out of the car when they got to the hotel. "You can sleep late if we don't have any kind of crisis," he said. "And, before I forget it, we'll want to set up another press conference—behind the scenes of course—when this Frithe goes on Trottingham's board. We'll work with the PR people at his bank. If he has any. See you guys."

Suzanne Kendrick had just glanced at her watch again when the phone rang. "Gary! I was just starting to wonder where you were."

She listened to the reasons for his being late. "I understand. Yes, of course I want to see you, turkey. I'm all dressed and ready to come pick you up. Why don't I do that? We can have a drink in the bar there; it's not so crowded this time of night. The boat people? Oh, I forgot, but even so, shall I? I'll be there in twenty minutes. For me? Uh, a daiquiri."

Suzanne checked herself before the mirror before she left. Everything was in place, looked good if not altogether genuine. Okay, Sooz, she told herself as she started the Datsun, let's get it on.

Outerbridge let Levy and Brooks out at the Dock Street Disco. Across the street, now tied to the wharf were the *Atlantis III*, the *Kungsholm* and the *Doric*, all bathed in floodlights. Brooks and Levy bought their tickets and handed them to the two gigantic men who framed the entrance. Music pounded at them; strobe lights flickered rapidly, making them momentarily dizzy. People danced on the floor and on the rug that surrounded it; it seemed to Levy that something was forcing them to move to the music. "My god," he said. "Look at the women!"

"Yeah, I see, but let's get some place where we can breathe. Like the bar. How many fuckin' decibels is that thing set to? Jeese!"

They forced their way between the tourists to the bar.

"Wow," Brooks said when they finally were able to get their elbows upon it. "I wonder which of our boys owns this joint." He glanced in the mirror at an angle and saw Fern Cromwell at precisely the same time she saw him. Mandarino had told them he'd seen her last week, but they'd all assumed she'd be back in Washington by this time. He pulled Levy to him. "Hey Kevin. There's Fern Cromwell from NBC and she's on her way—Fern!" he greeted her. He kissed and embraced her, looking past her at the slender, oval-faced girl with light brown hair. Something in her eyes made her older than she looked. "Heard you were here," he said.

"I wonder who told you," she said. "And who's this, Kevin? Ah, yes, Kevin. Remember me?"

"How could I forget?" Cromwell had almost blown the campaign they were handling for Congressman McClintock when she reported his apprehension by D.C. cops at a whorehouse in the ghetto.

"And," Levy said to Churchill, "who are you?"

"Linda Churchill, *Berhama Times.*" She extended her hand.

Levy took it. "You work for that rag?"

"We all have to work somewhere. You work with Mandarino, don't you?"

Brooks said, "Are you running a story tomorrow on the meeting?"

"What meeting?" Churchill asked.

Cromwell turned away, laughing.

"The one you sent the photographers to," Levy said, signalling a bartender.

Brooks was quickly trying to calculate how much they'd had to drink and how much they could get from them and most important, how much information they already had. It was probably a good decision they'd made to go public within the next day or so.

"Oh," Churchill said, laughing, "*that* meeting."

"What're you folks drinking?" Levy asked, holding the bartender by his sleeve so he would not go away. Levy was shouting. They were all shouting.

"Gin and tonic without the tonic," Cromwell said. She was snapping her fingers to the music and weaving her body.

"How about you, little lady?" Brooks said to Churchill.

"Double vodka and ginger."

"What time's it?" Cromwell asked.

Brooks looked at his watch. "Midnight."

"Shit," Cromwell said.

"What's wrong?"

"I had a date fifteen minutes ago, Mike."

"Better hurry."

She shook her head, still moving. "Uh-uh. I found somethin' better." She kissed Brooks on the mouth.

"No shit?" Brooks said.

"No shit, papa."

The drinks came and Levy, having a sudden inspiration told the bartender, "The same all around, but make it doubles." He watched Brooks seize his scotch with the same eagerness he had seized his own.

"I am distressed," Levy said, moving closer to Churchill, "that you haven't asked any questions. Do you know all the answers?"

"Did you know all the answers when you worked on the St. Louis *Post-Dispatch*?"

Levy took a long look at Churchill before he attacked his drink again.

"Did Mike know all the answers when he was with the *Washington Post*?" You're good-looking," she said.

"You've been hanging around with Cromwell too long. Did you meet down here or—"

"Berhama is the cross-roads of the world, Kevin Levy. Everything that happens bigger elsewhere, happens in small here."

"I'm not good at riddles."

"At dancing?" She took his hand and led him to the floor. "Enjoy it," she said, moving into a hip-snapping, breast bouncing routine. "I'm tired of asking and tired of knowing."

Levy was into his thing, a cunning routine with the feet, elbows and shoulders. "I know what you, uh mean, Linda. Yeah!"

Back at the bar, Brooks was saying, "You're lookin' good, Fern. How's Capitol Hill treating you these days?"

"Listen man, if people knew, really knew, about the turkeys who run government, they'd all pack up and move to Outer Mongolia. But Mike, what the hell are you guys doin' down here? The election? What're the stats? We gonna have another riot this Christmas?"

"Hey, look. We got the account for the election. But you know the way we operate. Dock Street may be jivin', but they gotta get their act together if they want to win. There are hard stats; we don't work without them. But if you've been here for a week you know as well as we do that the problems come from within, not from without, the Berhama United Party."

"Will Gary do an interview with me?"

"No."

"I can make it nasty for him."

Brooks laughed. "Honey, don't start anything you can't handle."

Cromwell grinned. "Ah, yes. Well. Let's put it another way. I can help his man."

Brooks ordered some more drinks. "That's better," he said.

"Trottingham, right?"

"Naturally."

"But you got problems I have to cover."

"What problems? I mean we're dealing in fact, not fiction, Fern."

Cromwell sipped from the fresh drink. She looked at the dance floor. She frowned and continued to scan it as she spoke. "The polls. Trottingham is way down. The issues. Black and white. The Russians. Us. The economy."

Her words, each of them tumbled inside Brooks like stones into an empty well; they resounded. He considered them, then said, "How do you know?"

"Ways."

Now Brooks scanned the dance floor and did not

see Levy nor the girl with the Cockney accent, Churchill. "From her?"

"We worked together. Let's go. They're gone."

Brooks took a big swallow. "Where?"

"The hotel. They're probably heading for his room."

"So what? Is this supposed to be a gang bang?"

Cromwell finished her drink and grasped his arm. "Why not?"

TWELVE

"I know it's an awkward hour," Phipps apologized when Peter Frithe arrived at the small, dark bar between Wellington and St. Gregory's. "I was in bed myself," he said, shaking Frithe's hand which had been extended more in habit than in sincerity. "But, I was deluged with a bunch of shit the Prime Minister wished to have disposed of with some dispatch. Drink, Peter?"

"Oh hell, why not. What time's it?"

"Twelve-thirty, lad. Scotch was it? Right."

Frithe waited until he had taken a goodly swallow of his drink and until Phipps, who sometimes carried about him the theatre of the highlands, was ready to speak.

"Brrrr," Phipps said. He had finished his own drink and was now signalling for another. "Now, Peter. Would you consider taking a position on the board of directors of Trottingham's bank?" Phipps turned back to the bar as if to provide privacy for Frithe.

Frithe studied the back of Phipps' head. He smiled. He drank.

"My, my, my," he said. "Aren't we all cloak and dagger and Scotland Yard."

Phipps turned to look at him; he shrugged his shoulders.

"Rhetorically, Phipps, what's in it for me?"

"Now man," Phipps said, "you have lots of canny Scots blood in you; need we go into that? Need we go into the obvious? That Trot-Trot needs you more than you need him?" Phipps shook his head sadly. "After what they did to you, my friend, they owe you far more than they're offering at the moment."

It will appear to some that peace has been made Frithe thought; that black union radicalism has gone the usual route. If I say yes, that'll help with the election: help them. But how will it help me and the people of Berhama? Suppose instead of remaining an independent, I joined the BUP? And suppose, whether or not the party wished it, I ran for a seat and won, became a member of Parliament? Would Trottingham dare not put me in his Cabinet? And from there, where could I go, what could I do? Frithe said, "I assume from the hour that my answer is being waited on?"

Phipps said dryly, "What a remarkable conclusion, Peter. Really quite marvelous." He ducked and laughed as Frithe took a slow swing at his head. "In this place," Phipps said, calling for still another drink, "expediency has always blurred the vision of most. But you, Peter, are not a rash man. Never were. Never will be."

"It's the combination of Scots and African blood, Phipps."

"Perhaps, lad." Phipps looked at his watch.

"Don't rush me," Frithe said. "Another drink."

Phipps sighed and ordered.

"You going to the boat party tomorrow?" Frithe asked.

"Fuck the boat party. No." Phipps replied. "The goddamn thing's a disgrace. Nothing points more to the racial division on this island than that folderol."

"I'll do it," Frithe said.

"What?"

"I'll do it, Phipps." Frithe swallowed his new drink.

"That's great," Phipps said, taking his hand.

"Can I include you in my plans?"

Phipps laughed loudly. "A true Scot, by God: already scheming. Yes, Peter, here's my hand on it." He laughed again.

Not a true Scot, Frithe thought, or I would have found a way to keep the money Graham gave me the other night and do this as well. Now, I have to give it back. But I *will* have some fun before I do.

"Who's that with Levy?" Mandarino had asked, more to himself than to Suzanne Kendrick. The Settlers' Bar had thinned out. They sat in a corner where they could watch people passing back and forth across the lobby.

"Not bad, whoever she is," Suzanne had said.

Soon after, they saw Brooks walk quickly through the lobby to the elevator.

"I wonder what his hurry is?" Mandarino said.

"Maybe he's joining Kevin."

"Uh-uh. That's not his style. But something's up."

Up the back stairs treading softly over the carpet, Fern Cromwell had raced. It had been necessary for her to avoid the front desk and to stay away from her room. Archibald might have been in one place or the other.

"Hungry?" Mandarino asked.

"You?"

"Yeah, I could eat a good steak. Know of a place?"

"They serve late at the Trafalgar. On the water."

"Let's go."

They walked holding hands. Dock Street was softer now at the dark beginnings of the morning. They walked close together, occasionally rubbing shoulders or hips.

"There goes the Canterbury Hook ferry," she said.

"The Staten Island Ferry is prettier," Mandarino said. "And probably cheaper."

"You'll always be a New Yorker, Gary."

"What's wrong with that?"

Suzanne didn't answer. She walked saucily now, stopping now and again to smile at Mandarino and to pull him close. "Hey," she said. "Didn't you want Kevin and Mike to see me? See how fat I've become? Ashamed of me?"

Now Mandarino stopped. "You saw those guys.
Like hunters—" and here he imitated their walks
through the lobby, "—closing in on the kill. Look,
they didn't wanna see *me*."

"Were you ever like that?"

"Who me? Never." Mandarino was glad that
they had arrived in front of the Trafalgar. "Here
we go."

The garden was hushed except for the waves
lapping at its seawall. Now and again a voice
reached them from the street, carried on the wind.
The light flickered in the orange jar in which the
candle sat.

"Romantic," she said.

"Yeah." He took her hands. "How you doin',
babes, okay?"

"All right." She was rubbing her thumbs over
the backs of his hands. "Can't you tell?"

Mandarino kissed her. "Yeah. Gee, kid, you look
awfully good."

"So do you. Did Stu ever tell you that he thought
you'd make a good male model?"

"C'mon."

"For the 'before and after commercials'. You'd
be before." She laughed and kissed him, noticing
as she did that the waiter had arrived.

"How about some champagne?" Mandarino asked.

Suzanne Kendrick pretended to consider it, then agreed.

When the waiter had taken their order and gone, she said, "Who're you seeing, Gary?"

"I'm not seeing anybody, Sooz."

"Don't have time. I know. A New Yorker like you. Is she nice?"

Mandarino was warmed by the teasing, but he knew that she knew all the answers.

"She's nice. Haven't seen her in quite a while, though. We just got back together."

Suzanne caught herself. She hadn't really meant it and—then she understood.

"Maybe she had a couple of big problems. Or medium-sized ones."

"Everybody has problems," Mandarino said, watching the waiter pour the champagne. "Here's to you, Sooz." They touched glasses.

"Gary," she said. "Are you planning to stay with me tonight?"

Mandarino looked up, trying to see the sudden, sharp crackle of desperation reflecting from her voice to her face. He saw nothing.

"That's up to you, Suzanne." Mandarino compressed his lips. Sooz would be coming up with an excuse. That's why her voice sounded so strange, he thought.

"God, I want you to." She turned slightly away from him. "I want you to. I was so afraid that you wouldn't be able to; that you might have to work."

"Kevin and Mike . . . they do the work. I'm the thinker, remember?"

She lowered her forehead until it touched his wrists. "Once," she said, "we only had to look at each other, or tell from the way one of us moved, that it was time to go bed. And now we have to talk about it." She raised herself. "I guess that's my fault."

"I noticed that you've been behaving like Mother Earth."

"Never mind. I'm happy now. Eat your steak."

The waiter was Portuguese. "Enjoy your dinner," he said.

And hurry up, Mandarino imagined him thinking, when he had poured more wine and left. It is late.

"Have to get up early?"

"Naw. You've got a phone. Without phones we'd be dead. I'm all right."

Halfway through the meal, Suzanne said, "I'm thinking about going back in a couple, three weeks."

"Fantastic," Mandarino said. "Let's live together."

"Only that?" Suzanne arched her brows.

"You may decide that even that's too much, babes."

"And you?"

"Yeah. Me too."

"And suppose it works."

"I dunno. I guess we get into the paper routine, no?"

"Well."

"That's all? Well? You know, all this time I figured you and Rafe were doing okay. I heard about the agency. Thought about stopping in. But, you hadn't gotten in touch with me, and I took that as a hint, you know, always remembering the great times we'd had, never forgetting them, measuring other people up to those times. And now, boom. No more Rafe. You're hiding out down here. I see you and the old drum goes bomma-booma-booma, and I think to myself: hey, you're not a kid anymore; here's a second time around, better, too, Sinatra says, and kid, you look great, and yeah I want to be with you tonight. And every night."

Suzanne was silent for a moment, then she said, softly, removing all the sarcasm from it, inserting love instead, "Wow."

Mandarino said, grinning, "Dynamite copy, huh?"

"Really."

There was a softness about the hour, about the island, when they arrived at her cottage. At the door she paused and sighed, then opened it. Closing it behind him, she looked intently into his eyes. "There's champagne in the refrigerator," she said. "Why don't you get it? I'll meet you in the bedroom."

Mandarino looked around for a phone. He saw it. "Okay, Sooz, but let me call Levy to make sure they're at work. Then I'll—" he paused to kiss her, "—come on in."

It took several minutes to go through the hotel switchboard, and then several minutes, it seemed, before Levy answered.

"You guys working on that statement?"

"Uh, Gary, we don't have to worry about that for tomorrow."

"Why not?"

"Everything's okay. Day after."

"How come you're so sure?"

"Somebody from the paper told me."

"That babe you were rushing through the lobby with?"

"Aggh, er—"

"Yeah?"

"Yeah."

"What's Mike doin'?"

"Tryin' to get some sleep like me, I hope."

"Fuck you. What's he doin'? He shacked up, too?"

"I dunno. Hey, where're you? In the hotel?"

"I'm with Sooz."

There was a long pause and Mandarino thought he heard a rustling of sheets and a giggle.

"How's she? What's she doin' here?"

"She's great and—"

"Oh yeah. Gary. Fern Cromwell—you know, NBC—is here and she wants to do something with Trotts."

"Okay. When? I didn't know she was still down here. We have to see what it is she wants, though." And then Mandarino had a thought. "Didn't Mike used to have the hots for her when he was with the *Post*?"

"Huh?"

"Come off it, Kevin. Is that where he is now? Jesus. I turn my back for a second and you guys're runnin' off in every direction gettin' laid instead of taking care of the job at hand."

"This *is* the job at hand, Gary. Listen, I'm goin' back to sleep. What time'll you be around tomorrow?"

"When I get there. You and Mike handle the Cromwell thing, and have some ideas for that statement."

"Tell Sooz we said hello."

"We?"

"Me and Mike."

"You guys holding what they used to call an orgy there?"

"You wanna come? With Sooz?"

"Fuck off." Mandarino hung up and, humming and loosening his tie, went for the champagne.

"In here, Gary."

Mandarino thought her voice sounded a little tentative.

Using the light of the half moon, he moved across the bedroom and found a table beside the bed. "Nice," he said. He smelled the ocean and the foliage, her scents of powder and perfume. He passed her a glass. "Careful. It's kind of full."

"Got it," she said, almost in a whisper. Their fingers brushed:

Mandarino undressed, knowing he was silhoutted against the window. He wondered why she had bothered to put a gown on. He sat down heavily on the side of the bed and took his own glass. "I can't tell you how great it is to be with you," he said. "Honest."

"I have kind of a great feeling, too, Gary."

"Talking to Kevin, I had the feeling that everyone on this island is doing it tonight."

She laughed easily. "That's what they say. It's better in Berhama."

Mandarino poured again, emptying the split. He said, "Somehow, Sooz, this doesn't seem to be *you*; know what I mean? Here, alone. I think of you together with Fifth Avenue, touch football players in the fall in Central Park, the Empire State Building, New York, cocktail parties, beautiful people."

"Yes. I think of you the same way, babes."

Mandarino finished his wine in a gulp and carefully set it down. Just as carefully, he took her glass and set it down and, conscious of the warm breeze playing upon his naked body, he swung over in the bed and cradled Suzanne in his arms as she issued a little gasp.

"What's the matter?"

He didn't wait for her answer. He kissed her and felt her responding, and his hands moved over her body which seemed to him to both retreat and advance to meet his touch until at last, her movements were all toward him, bold, eager, abandoned. Mandarino grasped the hem of her short gown and pulled it upward. "Off with this," he murmured.

Suzanne let him slip the gown from her then lay back and watched him, his shadow as it moved toward her then stopped. She felt his hands plucking tentatively at the band around her mutilated breasts. She cradled his face in her hands, heard him whisper.

"What's this stuff? Take it off."

She felt a dam rising quickly against her passion, felt a bewilderment enter Mandarino's movements. Suzanne Kendrick's legs had been opened, quivering, awaiting his entrance, knees up. Now she let her legs collapse down on the bed with a soft sound and, still cradling his face said," "They're gone, babes. Both of them. You know, cancer—"

And Mandarino stilled his movements for a second and listened to the words echoing and re-echoing in his head, and then he knew why she was here, why she was sad, why she'd worn the gown. And he knew too, suddenly, as lightning flashing soundlessly across the sky before its noise comes, that if he did not continue with his lovemaking she would be hurt beyond a summons at a later time from anyone, especially himself. Her world, at least as she saw it at the moment, would exist only if he could overcome whatever revulsion she thought he might have. It was not the princess kissing the frog to turn it into the handsome prince; this time out it was the prince's turn. He felt tears gather in his eyes, felt them running onto her hands, felt those hands growing both more tender and passionate. With soft sobs she brought his face close to hers, now also growing wet, and they lay for a moment motionless. Then he kissed her long and hungrily, exploring her mouth positioning his own upon it, as a lifeguard would do when applying mouth-to-mouth resuscitation to someone pulled drowning from the sea; and she, as if responding to his oxygen, sobbed and cried sharply into the night in time with movements of her body now rising to the insistent beat of passion.

And he entered her in full gallop and her soul sighed that he had been able to.

And so did his.

THIRTEEN

At half-past twelve Sinclair Archibald had given up phoning room 520, given up lurking in the corridors where every passing janitor and waiter knew what he was doing or, rather, who he was waiting for.

There was in progress a party in the Bendersen suite and word had already drifted down to him that Cynthia was not there and, in fact, had not even been invited. It was a party composed of the people who thought they were, or were on the edge of becoming, beautiful. They were asteroids attracted to Bendersen's star, and they radiated in his presence which was itself vibrated by the top-volume playing of his latest hits.

Archibald knew nothing of music, nothing of show business, but it had always seemed to him that Cynthia took herself far too much for granted. She had none of the steel Archibald suspected public people must have; she was malleable plastic and that had attracted him to her. He had not known that she had not known, and therefore never could have made, the distinction between plastic and steel.

Cyhthia Archibald sprang to the phone before it had completed its first ring. It was not that she was overly concerned with the sound waking her parents and her child; rather, she thought that it might be Sandy Lapidus calling to invite her to a party. All over the island there were parties in honor of the last leg of the race tomorrow. Even though people might have been untouched by the event, they nevertheless seized upon it as an opportunity to party only because so many other Berhamians were. She had not heard from Sandy in a day.

"I want to talk to you and I'm coming over," Archibald announced.

To his surprise she had said, "All right."

Cynthia had pushed the bags out of sight. She'd spent half the evening looking at them, seeing herself unpacking them and hanging her clothes in the closet of their sunbaked house in the center of the island. And as she did, a sense of dread had enveloped her. Sandy had said, indeed he had, that if he became too busy to see her while Bendersen was here, she should meet him at the eleven o'clock flight time tomorrow night. He would have her ticket. Then why the sense of dread, she kept asking herself. No shadows had been cast in their brief, explosive island reunion, just as none had been cast after their fling in New York; if something cast no shadow, it was not of this world. Cynthia Archibald felt as though she had missed some important beat in a piece of music. Was Sandy with someone else at this very moment? Why had he not asked her to meet Bendersen? Why had she not become a part of the Bendersen entourage that everyone was talking about? She sat, waiting. And now Sinclair had called and she was allowing him to come over and talk to her—and it was two in the morning.

The moped sounded unusally loud at that hour. Cynthia slipped out of the house and walked into the yard where Archibald was taking off his helmet. She saw him look at the car. He had not insisted on having it, the way most Berhamian men did under similar circumstances; for them a car was like another woman.

"Everybody asleep?" Archibald asked. He noticed that she was dressed and scented as if waiting to go out.

"At this hour, what else?"

Now he eyed her slowly then said, "Not everybody's asleep or about to go to sleep."

Cynthia Archibald became suddenly aware of what she was wearing. She said, "Well, I thought I would go out, but I changed my mind."

They walked away from the house down near the road upon which from time to time whined mopeds with their riders or cars whose drivers blasted through the speed limit. They sat on a bench beneath a poinsettia tree. It was the same bench they used to sit on when they were courting.

"How come you're not somewhere partying with Peter or some of the others, Sinclair?"

Archibald passed her a cigarette and lighted it for her and then lit one for himself. "I wanted to be here, and I wanted to talk to you. I was surprised that you said okay."

"I guess I was, too," she said.

A moped went by slowly, a boy and girl laughing into the still dark morning. With the breeze from the ocean came the scent of an array of flowers, like the perfume a young girl wears on her first date, hoping that it will attract, but not too much.

"How's David?"

"Okay."

"Your folks?"

"All right."

"Your father have anything to drink in there?"

"You know father. Want to come in?"

"No. Just bring about half a tall glass filled with anything. You drinking?"

Cynthia said, "Why not?"

Archibald heard her walking back toward the house. He remained where he was staring into the darkness out toward the sea. Once he had seen a map of the ocean floors. The island of Berhama, an ancient sea mount, was barely an orange dot among the rifts, submerged valleys and abyssal plains. How then was it that the world beat a track to this place, corrupting its isolation—their erstwhile Eden crude though it might have been—with all the disadvantages, but few of the benefits of its plunge through the 20th century? The world seemed to do that to all tropical islands and their inhabitants.

"What're you thinking?" Cynthia asked when she returned. She handed him a glass that was more than half full. He tasted it. Scotch. He saw that her glass, too, was very full.

"About us, I guess, and how we've got to stop being victims of tourists. We depend on them; that should be enough. We do need their money. We provide services for that. Even exchange, maybe. But girl; we've been giving them everything else." He did not say "our bodies," nor did he say "self-respect."

But Cynthia thought she understood. "Sinclair, tell me truthfully. Do you think I have real talent?"

Archibald didn't hesitate. "No. We've all humored you. We knew that you thought you had talent, but we also believed that after the Miss Berhama tour you'd come back and shake the star dust out of your eyes. For Christ's sake, Cynthia, billions of people in the world would've given their arm just to have done what you did, and they would have been willing to call it a day, content with the memory. Suppose your competition had been girls from the States. How far do you think you'd have gone in that contest?"

"You never said anything," she said. Her tone was sharp.

"You don't when it's someone you love."

"Crap."

"No it's not, and you know it. How many girls have we seen in Trinidad or Jamaica or Barbados or Grenada who've been beauty queens who sang a little? They're all hanging around bars, waiting for the celebrities to come in so they can be with them. And completely without warning, they let you know that they were Miss so-and-so. Ah, shit. I mean, I thought you learned from that."

207

"But you didn't have to go out that night and not come home!"

"Yes! You're right! I didn't have to. I shouldn't have. And you shouldn't have moved out. You were just waiting for an excuse. That's the way it looked to me and—" Why should he mention that man? She knew that he knew, just as she knew about Fern. "—this is no good, Cynthia. Let's get back together."

Cynthia sipped from her drink. She felt a sudden onset of relief. Once again her life was framed, secure; she could visualize it. She felt his arm around her and his shoulder pressing her gently back down upon the bench. She moved with the pressure, finding the ground with her glass and resting the drink upon it. She heard his glass clink softly upon the walk, too, and then she felt the breeze upon her legs, her thighs and she hoisted herself and felt him slip her step-ins off. For a moment he twisted and bent near her, then he was upon her and finally, in her.

(Inside the house Mr. Manley, having heard the murmur of the voices and now the silence punctuated by gasps that buffeted the night, turned to his wife and pulled her close to him. She woke sleepily, realized what was happening and said, "Uh!")

"I need to think about it." Cynthia Archibald was saying. They were sitting again, arm in arm.

But Archibald felt that he'd won. "I'll call you tonight," he said. "About midnight. From the hotel."

"All right. I'll really think about it, Sin."

"I know you will." By then, he thought, she will have had time to get back from the airport and get over her disappointment. He kissed her again and fastened on his helmet. He let the moped roll away from the house before starting it, then kicked it in and rode off humming.

H.M.S. *Dauntless* took up her position five miles off St. Gregory's Head, just as the eastern horizon went from black to blue and from blue to purple and from purple to a dull orange. The race officials, holding mugs of strong tea, were already on the bridge, their chests encrusted with binoculars.

One of the radiomen climbed the bridge and handed the captain a message. "Gentlemen, looks like a triumph for Berhama," he said. "A U.S. Navy plane tells us that a sloop has a big lead—about four hours."

"What's the name, captain?"

"I was just going to say—it's *Berhama Brave*. Do you know it?"

"I say," one of the judges said. "Isn't that young MacKenzie's craft?"

"Yes, it is," said another. The others thumbed through their lists.

"In any event," the captain said, "estimated arrival time is five hours. Ten o'clock this morning."

Five to fifteen hours northwest the ships came, here and there a single vessel, sails blown to the full, like the *Berhama Brave*, punched through the sea in near solitude; others, bunched like tangled, brightly-colored beads, put on more sail if they had it to spare and tried to break out. And then further up the rhumb line, there came a single and another single, then a few ships running like children about to be lost from the family, and then bunches of them again. Twenty ships had dropped out with split sails and no spares, or had capsized, or had fallen so far behind that their crews decided to slow down and party all the way into Berhama.

But on they came, *Motola*, *Roig* and *Dasher*; knifing through the bluing waters in the low flat rays of the rising sun came *Hero*, *Old Woman* and *Daphne*; crashing and burning in the stretch ran *Triumphant*, *Water Bird* and *Sea Hawk*; the exhausted crews of *Fleet Wind*, *Don Jaime* and *Big Apple* urged their creaking, bounding vessels on with rope and sail and weight.

The *Rotterdam*, returning from St. Thomas and giving wide berth to the rhumb line, signalled with her whistle; she would be in port in a berth in Wellington long before even *Berhama Brave* and her passengers would be walking up and down Dock street by noon.

Working fishermen maneuvered their crafts out along the reefs where during the course of the day they hoped to catch rockfish, red snapper, yellowtail snapper and gray snapper. Game fishermen rode their motor launches out farther, looking for Wahoo, Yellowfin tuna, Dolphin, Great Barracuda, Blue Marlin and Almaco jack. All would watch for the first spark of color from the sails of the ships in the fleet.

Queen Hotel employees, just as the hotel people at the Royal Berhamian and fifty other guest establishments around the island, began arriving at their jobs on foot, by moped and by car. In Wellington only the Queen and the Royal Berhamian hotels, however, flew ships' flags on lanyards above their marquees.

In the barracks of the Berhama Regiment, soldiers went over their red dress uniforms, brushed lint from them, flicked cloths over the already brightly burnished buttons and checked the trouser creases. Today they would be on parade.

Summerall hurried down the basement stairs of the Consulate to the coding room. He did that every morning. It was routine.

211

Berhama customs officials arrived at their assigned parking places on Dock Street near the berth where the *Rotterdam* would pull in. Out in the harbor two tugs, their hung-over crews drinking black coffee, bobbed in the tide and waited for the gigantic vessel to arrive.

Ten panel trucks bearing in Gothic letters the legend: *Read The Berhama Times,* raced around the island dropping off their bundles of the paper.

Linda Churchill turned over in Kevin Levy's bed and groaned. She had a hangover.

Levy slept on.

So did Mike Brooks, stretching out in his bed now that Fern Cromwell had leaped out of it.

The station manager, who lived out in McDuffy district, hopped out of his bed with the first blast of the horn of the studio truck. He would ride with the crew into Wellington, pick up Cromwell and accompany her around the town until ten, when she would interview the Prime Minister. The station manager did not like having such complex arrangements made so late in the evening with people who were obviously drunk. Still, the woman was from *network*; the thing had to be done.

Cromwell jiggled in the ice cold shower. She sang a spiritual uptempo, or tried to, as she mentally picked the wardrobe she would wear today. "I know the Lor-or-ord, I know the Lor-or-ord, I know the Lor-or-ord's laid his hands on me!"

Outerbridge sat in the Humber picking his teeth and listening to the bird sounds; he liked Berhama best when it was just between waking and sleeping. Down on the Trottingham front lawn, he heard the gardener snipping at shrubs; when he was certain the Trottinghams were up, he would start the lawn mower.

Inside, Greta Trottingham listened to the gardener and slowly pulled herself atop her husband, submitting to his positioning hands. She thought about the man in the garden.

Moments later, Kirkland Trottingham rushed to his shower, pausing a moment to study his calendar. He smiled. He was going to be on American television.

Graham Rattery awoke with a rushing sound in

his head and a pounding in his chest. He was sweating.

Sandy Lapidus carefully unhooked himself from the middle of a clutch of sleeping nude female bodies. He knew that after the performance they would all parade to the airport, high and tired, but still beautiful people, and take the plane back to New York where each would go his or her separate way to recuperate for a day or two before heading out to do the West Coast tour. Then this would start all over again.

In a borrowed car, Peter Frithe, still yawning, picked up Clarence, Clifford and Claretson for the drive out to St. Gregory's. The sun seemed to be coming up fast now, and from the channel he heard the blast from the horn of the *Rotterdam*. By the time he got back to Wellington, it would be already tied up along Dock Street.

All three wore their red, green and yellow caps. They were more somber than usual. On the way, it seemed to Frithe that they looked at things more intensely than they ever had. He wondered how he would have felt at their ages had he been faced with their tasks this morning.

The radio announced the sighting of *Berhama Brave*; it announced the party to be held at the Royal

Berhamian Hotel in the afternoon, with Jax Bendersen playing; then came the news of the world and music. Frithe lit another cigarette. It was pleasant driving without conversation; it was like being alone.

He glanced in the mirror at Clarence and Clifford; Claretson was sitting beside him. Did they, he wondered, see themselves at the barricades, young leaders of an explosive revolution? Did they see themselves disco-ing from the end of ropes? Did they see themselves as men-in-waiting to Premier Rattery?

They drove through St. Gregory's and out past Ramada Inn. Now the three youths looked with quick interest at the terrain as Frithe eased off the hard road onto a dirt trail. He shifted into first gear. The foliage snapped and slid along the car.

"This is as far as we can go," Frithe said. "Leave the doors open."

Clarence, Clifford and Claretson got out and looked around. Frithe pointed through the leaves. "The Ramada," he said. Brightly-colored pennants were flying from the roof. "Come on."

They showed only mild surprise at the stone house. They waited, bunched together, until Frithe had unlocked the door and casually waved them in. "This is where I kept the grenades," he said and, as the last of the three entered, he quickly closed the door and locked it and shot the bolt.

Frithe walked around to the window. He had
boarded it up and affixed a pair of sturdy old shutters to it. He heard only a murmur from inside,
though he was sure that, had the door and window
been open, he would have heard shouting and
cursing—one of the rare times any true noise was
ever heard from their collective voices.

Continuing around the house, Frithe pulled the
knapsack with the grenades from a hiding place.
He looked at the window again as he passed it,
checked the lock on the shutters. Then he tested
the door and went off to the car. He laughed to
himself. Clarence, Clifford and Claretson were not
pounding at the door or window. Perhaps they
were sitting on the floor not hearing, seeing or
speaking. During the course of the day, however,
he was sure they would find the sandwiches and
beer he'd left in a corner. When he let them out
tonight they would find the same Berhama they'd
left because the changes would not be immediately
visible and in any case, would take a little time.

Frithe eased over the bumpy trail back to the
hard road and Wellington.

FOURTEEN

Mandarino awoke to the sound of the shower. He lay still trying to imagine what she looked like with her breasts gone. Perhaps he would never see the places where they'd been. He wondered why it was that men, of all the animals, seemed to be most attracted to the female breast.

"Get up, you bum," she said when she came out, walking through the bedroom to the kitchen, "but not until I bring you some juice to take into the shower."

Mandarino grinned. She remebered that. "What time's it, Sooz?"

"Eight."

Mandarino showered and dressed. In the kitchen, with a cup of coffee before him, he called the hotel.

"So what's the drill, Mike?"

"We're working on the statement." Brooks and Levy, with three pots of coffee, an assortment of rolls, sausages, bacon and kippers, together with cold boiled eggs and juices and a rented typewriter, sat in their shorts. "It's almost done. It'll be finished by the time you get here."

"Yeah, yeah. Anything more on that Frithe deal?"

"He's doin' it," Brooks said. "Phipps called us about an hour-and-a-half ago, so we're getting that ready, too. Phipps has all the details and he's due over any minute."

"This Cromwell babe; what's she want?"

"No problem, Gary. She's out right now getting some wild stuff with the local people. They furnished a truck, sound man and cameraman. She sees Trotts at ten. Her pitch will be the celebration of the free enterprise system; the boat race'll be all these money grubbers having a little fun. Trotts'll come over as a steady hand on the ship of state. She'll do the boat party later, too—"

"*When* did you decide to do all this, while you were shacked up?"

218

"Ah, uh, Gary, we just had an all night conference. It's okay though, right?"

Mandarino chuckled. "Listen, kid, I couldn't have done better sober. How about the press conference?"

"Kevin's working with Phipps on that. We thought we'd better have it tomorrow, even with the boat business, so it can come out the day after.

" 'kay."

"Wait. Kevin wants to say something."

"C'mon, Kevin. My coffee's gettin' cold."

"How's Sooz?"

"All right. What's up?"

"Phipps tells me that the king of Abu Dabi will be in next week."

"Uh-huh. What the hell's Abu Dabi?"

"Oil. Up the gig. Smells like mucho bread for Berhama."

"Hey, that's good for the BUP and Trottingham. Prosperity."

"Zackly."

"We get something together, right?"

"Trotts would like that. I guess that means staying a few more days or coming back next week."

"Maybe. Who was the babe?"

"What babe?"

"Last night."

"Oh. Well, that was Linda Churchill, you know, from the paper."

"Hey, Kevin. I like the way you guys work. Y'got style and it's improving all the time. She say how come they're always down on our boys?"

"The usual. Siggonson's brother and the working papers, you know. They produce or get fired."

"She gonna be on our side now?"

"I guess. We gotta get back to work. When you gonna be here? About an hour? That's good, because we're supposed to run a quick session by Cromwell and make sure she knows what we'd like her to do."

"Why's she so cooperative?"

"She knows where the power is, babes."

Levy hung up and said to Brooks, "Where were we?"

Mandarino finished his coffee and held his cup for another. He smiled at Kendrick. He wondered if the doctors had got it all, if she lived in fear that they had not. "Y' look good, kid," he said. "I don't want to leave you. Why don't you hang out with us today? We can make you script girl or something."

Suzanne smiled the old smile Mandarino remembered. "Really? I wouldn't be in the way?"

"Listen, you know those two. I'll be the only one without a girl to talk to today. And today is the big party day on the island. How about it?"

"Sure. Love to. It'll be my first party day in quite a while."

"Stick with me, babes, and you can party every day."

"Sure, while you're holding hands with congressmen, senators and governors and prime ministers. Sure."

"I'll hold your hand with my free hand."

"It sounds very, very nice, babes. We'll see. What'll I wear?"

"Just be comfortable, that's all."

She got up. "You got a deal, hot shot. I'll only be a minute. Then we can hit the road."

"I gotta call the office." Mandarino reached for the phone. Suzanne vanished into her bedroom to dress.

221

Linda Churchill looked at the glossy photos on her desk. One showed Gary Mandarino, his arm pointing toward Trottingham, MacKenzie, DeSilva, Donnelly and a host of other BUP members and Parliamentarians, with Levy and Brooks just behind him, sitting at a small table. She knew that the cap would read something like: PR MAN DIRECTS CABINET MEMBERS. Directs, orders, commands—the cap plainly would suggest that the Berhama government was in the charge of Mandarino and his associates.

The other revealed Trottingham in close-up, a puzzled expression on his face: CONFUSED PRIME MINISTER HANDS BERHAMA OVER. Bewildered, confused, confounded—this cap would imply a shaky hand at the helm of government.

Churchill pushed them both aside and went back to her story. The real story. The interview with Lapidus was already written. It was a piece of fluff passing as human interest, a subliminal salute to Berhama and the "class" visitors it attracted.

Churchill glanced over the lead again:

At a secret, after-dark meeting in the palatial home of Douglas MacKenzie, M.B.E., the mysterious public relations advisor to the Berhama United Party night before last was revealed as Gary Mandarino of Mandarino Associates of New York.

She and Levy had agreed that that information would be forthcoming in a statement anyway. And

222

add Levy and Brooks to the story. Churchill scribbled a reminder. She looked at her notes. Donnelly and DeSilva, among a dozen others, had called as soon as she'd arrived in the office fresh from Levy's bed. All had information on what had been said at the meeting, but the emphasis from person to person differed. The photographers had been too nervous to really listen.

But they all seemed to agree on one point:

Mr. Mandarino denied to the assemblage of BUP officials and Parliamentarians that his firm was attempting to dictate to Prime Minister Trottingham and his Cabinet.

Mr. Mandarino was accompanied by two associates, Mr. Michael Brooks and Mr. Kevin Levy.

It was this public relations organisation that conducted the highly controversial poll two months ago. The results of the poll, with its questions concerning the major political figures on the island, have never been made public.

Now Churchill looked up and across the office into the glass-enclosed area where Siggonson sat in dark suit, white shirt and gray tie, looking like a Fleet Street publisher. No. She would not use the figures. That sonofabith, she thought, would detonate the island. She was not going to give him the powder to do it. She pushed back from the typewriter and rapped her pencil against her teeth. Perhaps she ought to tell him, before Phipps calls, that a statement would soon be issued concerning Mandarino Associates and their work in Berhama. The meeting last night could be built around that.

Churchill looked at the clock. Ten. Would her headache never leave? It was time for another cup of coffee—and two more aspirin. She thought then about MacKenzie's offer to set her up with a paper. It sounded good. And she could see herself managing it. Even if she could get the reporters, however, she would be competing directly with the *Times*. MacKenzie would expect her to turn a profit right away; for members of Dock Street, quick profit was the essence of everything. Not that she didn't agree with MacKenzie's social policies; they were all right, though he really didn't know his troops. DeSilva and Donnelly played to what they considered his weakness and, at the first opportunity they would deliver disaster. And if she ran a paper, she would be right in the middle of it, beholden once again, not to her own skills, but to the whims of MacKenzie or whoever else he trusted.

Churchill gagged on the aspirin, got them down. Maybe, she thought, Europe wouldn't be so bad this time around. She would write a book, to hell with the newspapers. The idea greatly appealed to her. Europeans loved novels about the tropics, with all the sex and drinking and political shenanigans.

"Well," Mandarino was saying, looking past the camera, "we always give it our best shot. We come across as being involved with the candidate but that's only partly true; we're more concerned with the issues."

To Cromwell he said, "Okay, babes, that's enough. You've got to see Trottingham."

"That was good, Gary. Glad you changed your mind."

"I hear you know something about the poll stats," Mandarino said, watching the cameraman close down. "Do me a favor and don't use them now, okay?"

"What's in it for me?"

"Your job, honey. We owe you one for the McClintock campaign."

They were walking across the lawn to the Cabinet Building. "You wouldn't," Cromwell said, but her tone implied her complete unconcern.

"I'd try. Hey, how you and Mike gettin' on?"

"We're working journalists," she laughed. "That *is* Suzanne Kendrick with you, isn't it?" she whispered.

"Yeah."

"You've got better taste than I would have guessed, Gary. What's happened to her? How come she doesn't model anymore? I mean, she's a little hefty but, Christ, when you look at Jane Russell—"

"Got her own agency, Fern. But listen: what we'd like to come through is the steady hand. Responsible. Reliable. Honest. I know he's stiff. Give him the easy questions on integration—the whole idea scares the shit outa him, and he's still picking his way. We won't use any tight shots. Those pop-eyes of his make him look surprised or frightened. You turn this over good for us and I'll make it up to you. We're taking on a couple of new accounts you might be interested in."

"Pennsylvania Avenue?"

Mandarino smiled. "Not yet, maybe never, if you run Cuba around the pool table."

"Cuba," Cromwell breathed. The station manager was sidling up, but she waved him away into the Cabinet Building behind the cameraman and the sound man. "Even Fidel. Next thing you know, you'll be handling Red China too."

"No, no, babes. Not *Red* China. The Peoples' Republic of China." Mandarino grinned. "Deal?"

"Deal, hotshot. We'd better get in."

Cromwell watched as Mandarino, Brooks and Levy sat Trottingham in a corner of his office against a background of soft brown drapes and pictures of his family. Deftly Mandarino set beside the Prime Minister pictures of black Berhamian officials, while Suzanne Kendrick applied makeup. Mandarino checked through the camera. "More light, Mike. Yeah, yeah. That's good. Bring up that picture of the Prime Minister and Donnelly. Good. Right there. Fern, sit down and let's see. Hit that forehead, Sooz, and the nose—"

"Not unless you've got Egyptian number four or Negro number one," Cromwell said.

Suzanne said, "No. This is my own stuff."

"It ain't likely to match then, is it sugar? Leave it, Gary. How's the framing?"

"Fine. Can you tell your man to ready for some cutaways?"

"Excuse me," Amanda said, tip-toeing into the room. "Mr. Desilva's here."

"Kevin," Mandarino said, "take care of that, will you?"

"That's to be done in the BUP office, not here," Trottingham said.

"We know," Levy said. "I just want Mr. DeSilva to go over the statement with me on the way over there, Mr. Trottingham. The press people'll be there at eleven."

"I see, I see."

"Join you in a half-hour," Brooks said.

"What about Peter Frithe?" Trottingham said.

"The statement's ready," Mandarino said. "But

we won't do it today, Kirkland. A little at a time. Stretch it out." He grinned at Cromwell. "A drop at a time, like the Chinese water torture."

Trottingham felt sure that he was missing something, but now he turned his attention to the woman beside him. She didn't look so bad for someone who'd fallen out of a building a week ago.

Mandarino dropped back from the camera and said to the man who seemed to be in charge of the crew, "Your people gonna cover that conference?"

"Uh—" the station manager balked, looking at Cromwell who was ignoring him. *This* was her thing. She didn't give a damn about a press conference, now.

Sensing the hunger in the man, Mandarino touched his shoulder, bent intently toward him. "It was originally scheduled for tomorrow, but we changed it to this morning so you'd have it for tomorrow. You know, you can *air* it tomorrow."

"I see," the station manager said. "And what is the conference about?"

Mandarino pulled a copy of the statement from his pocket. "Here. At Phipps' office, wherever that is." He turned back. "If we're ready Mike, let's shoot."

"Quiet," Brooks said as the station manager retreated to a corner and read the statement. He would have to send another crew. After all, he was going to spend the day with that woman, and it looked like a very long day indeed."

"I really thought I could depend on them," the hotel manager said petulantly.

"Have you called them?" His look blamed Frithe for their absence.

"Oh, yes," Frithe said. "Maybe they went out to meet the ships."

"But they were supposed to be here. Oh, bother. Peter, then I'll have to ask you to do your very best to take up the slack. I'll have to give you at least two more tables to serve."

"Mr. Wiggins, I believe I can manage. Don't you worry."

Mr. Wiggins walked away, surveying the line of white-topped tables down the length of the lawn of the Royal Berhamian Hotel and the bandstand at one end of it. Already "the boys" were setting the tables with refreshments: bottles upon bottles of scotch, gin, vodka and bourbon. Under each table were boxes filled with extra bottles. Under Frithe's table, soon to be joined by two more, in addition to the bottles, was his knapsack containing five hand grenades.

In a few hours, Frithe thought, nearly everyone in front of the tables would be white and everyone behind them, black. An incredible celebration of the status quo. He paused in arranging his stacks of plastic glasses to watch the others loading their tables. He had pushed for a standard fee for serving at such affairs when he ran the union. The members, afraid to lose the extra money, rejected his plan. Each made his separate deal with the hotel managers who took turns each year hosting the yacht race party. Now, off-duty bartenders, waiters and people who just needed the money competed with each other for a table to serve, and all wound up with very little, though they worked until they sweated completely through their white jackets.

Luis DeSilva stopped suddenly and sat down on a bench. They were passing through a park not far from Phipps' office. "I don't like the statement," DeSilva said.

Smiling, Levy sat down beside him. The trouble with all these guys, he thought, was that they truly believed they, each one of them, ran the government instead of Trottingham. And Trottingham let them get away with it. The fact that Mandarino Associates were working for the BUP was, after all, an airball which everyone had used for his or her own purpose. DeSilva, Donnelly, Siggonson on down the line, and Trottingham, too. Trottingham tried to place the firm between himself and his detractors within the party as well as outside it.

By announcing their presence, the firm would be

taking weapons out of the hands of nearly everyone involved. Maybe then they could proceed normally. DeSilva knew that he would be losing a weapon with which to attack Trottingham. Like others, he would no longer have to run to the phone to tell Siggonson's reporters that Mandarino's people were in town. Of course, he didn't like the statement.

DeSilva was already dressed in white shoes, white pants and a blue linen blazer over a white shirt with open collar. Who could tell by looking at him that he did not really belong to the yachting crowd?

"Well," Levy said. "You read the memo from the Prime Minister about your making the statement as is."

DeSilva laughed. "Sure. But, I still don't like it. And, by the way, who're you guys to come down here and tell us what to do?"

Levy sighed. "Mandarino went over that last night. You were there. You're talking bullshit now, DeSilva. Let's go and make the statement."

"And if I don't choose to?"

"We've already considered that and the option is that the Prime Minister will issue the statement together with another one." Levy fished in his pocket and brought out a folded paper. He handed it to DeSilva who saw at once that it was a copy.

He read it, folded it up, unfolded it again and read it. "Clever," he said. "Fuckin' clever." He handed it back to Levy.

DeSilva knew that if he didn't do the statement at the press conference, Trottingham would do a later one in which he would also announce that he had asked for the resignation of the Honorable Luis DeSilva, M.P., Minister without portfolio in charge of the Ministry of Information. That was what the folded paper was about. He would then just be the owner of supermarkets, nothing more. Luis De-Silva wanted to be more than that. Now he felt checked. At least for the time being. "Let's go," he said, and they both rose and walked briskly to Phipps office where a television crew was just entering.

Both DeSilva and Levy hurried more when they recognized Linda Churchill waiting at the door.

Berhama Brave cleared St. Gregory's Head to a blasting of horns and shouts from the nondescript fleet that met it. The crew broke champagne out of the locker and by the time they had tied up the ship, they were well on their way to being quite drunk. Other vessels began to appear on the horizon.

Light-headed, Sandy Lapidus strode through

crowded Dock Street until he came to the Royal Berhamian Hotel. He reached the lawn with its long line of tables, decided against a drink, and walked to the bandstand to check the wiring, the speakers and the equipment.

As he walked around the bandstand he saw emerging from the hotel a smartly-dressed, attractive black woman who looked somehow familiar. With her was a slight, bewildered-looking man, another younger man bearing a television camera on his shoulder and another man with a box strapped to a hand truck he was wheeling. All were sweating and they appeared to be angry as well. They were following the woman up and down the lawn. Lapidus called out: "Hello, are you from NBC?"

"I am," she snapped.

Lapidus jumped from the bandstand. "I'm Sandy Lapidus, Jax Bendersen's agent. The woman from the paper told me you'd be around."

Cromwell said under her breath, "Oh, shit." To Lapidus she said, "Ah, yes. We'll get some footage of your show."

"But I thought you wanted to talk to Jax—"

"—uh, yes, but—uh, what's his schedule?"

Lapidus brightened. "He's at the hotel now. We start here at four."

233

Cromwell said hopefully, "I can catch him in Washington, can't I?"

"Oh, not soon. We go into New York and then out to the Coast."

Cromwell was aware of the tired, angry and sweating men behind her. "I'll try," she said. "But you know the Prime Minister will make an appearance here—"

She saw Lapidus' disappointment.She chucked him under the chin. "But you're a nice boy. We'll do the footage and I'll do more in the states and we'll hook up for a real interview with Jax."

"An interview? Just you and him?"

"That's what I said, didn't I?" She started to move off again and said, "I'll see you later." To the station manager she said, "We'll try to get him to walk out through those doors, see, and then we can get the band in the background." She backed up, looking at the cameraman. "You back up as he comes toward you, a little *cinema verité*."

The cameraman gave a bored nod. *Cinema Merdé*, he thought.

"It's going to be very crowded," the station manager said. "You may have to change plans." He looked at his watch. "Time we got to St. Gregory's," he said.

"Shit, I'm hungry." The sound man by his look challenged anyone to say that he was not.

234

"Can we get something on the way?" Cromwell asked, annoyed.

The station manager wondered if the lunch would be coming out of network funds. "We're late as it is," he said.

"We'd better go then," Cromwell said, and she marched off back through the hotel, the sound man and the cameraman kicking angrily at the grass.

FIFTEEN

A few moments before four o'clock, the cooling breezes starting to blow in from the sea, the tourists on Dock Street paused to listen to sounds of rock music blaring out above the street through loudspeakers. From the Royal Berhama Yacht Club, where yachts, yawls, schooners and sloops were tying up every few minutes to the shouts of the crews and announcements over still other loudspeakers, the tourists saw blue-blazered men in white shoes, pants and shirts hurrying up to the Royal Berhamian Hotel, accompanied by women as tanned and blond as the men. Some were drunk, some sang, some shouted. All were happy.

The lawn before the hotel was filled with people who formed lines in front of the tables. White-jacketed bartenders grabbed and poured and spilled; spilled and poured and grabbed. The press to the serving tables was inexorable.

Jax Bendersen screamed into the microphone, played his guitar with long, fast fingers. He was high; he was feeling good, and so were his sidemen.

Sandy Lapidus watched them and was glad he'd had most of his good time before they got to Berhama, because it was going to be a mess getting them off the island. Why should he complain, though? They were making a lot of bread and expenses for a three-hour gig; he could recover later.

From one end of the lawn to the other, the talk was about times, sails, winds, crews, divisions. And Graham Rattery, four floors above the party, looked out and watched. Wall-to-wall money, he thought, uniformed in blue and white—except for the women, of course. He wondered why he had not seen Clarence, Clifford or Claretson. He saw Frithe, pouring away, shoving drinks blindly toward outstretched hands. He seemed to be having fun. Blasted band, he thought. But all would be okay with Frithe there.

Kirkland Trottingham was still unconvinced that making an appearance at the party would be good public relations. Where, he wondered, did that Italian get his ideas. But he had agreed, especially since that Cromwell woman would be there with a television crew.

"Well, Outerbridge," he said when he left his office and went to his car, "let's get this bloody thing over with."

Outerbridge smiled and held the door open for him. "I don't think it'll be so bad, Prime Minister."

Settling himself in the back, Trottingham said, "So, you've become an authority on these affairs, have you?"

"Sort of, Sir." Outerbridge smiled into the rearview mirror.

"Humph. Is Mrs. Trottingham in readiness for the deluge of drunks who will descend on my house in an hour or so?"

"I believe she is, yes, Sir."

"Did you get the rum?"

"Yes, I did."

Trottingham's eyes watched the fluttering flag of his office as they drove through the congested traffic. The traffic officers waved them through and saluted. Trottingham touched his forehead with his fingertips and snapped off returns. "Nice fellows," he said.

At the hotel parking lot he got out, looking for

Mandarino and his people. A motley crew he thought, when he sighted them bearing down on his car. Why that Churchill person was with them he did not know. And that other person with the camera—ah, yes, Corduro, one of Siggonson's photographers. Trottingham smiled broadly as Mandarino, Levy, Brooks, Suzanne Kendrick, Churchill and Corduro came up. "Ah, er, where is the television lady?" he asked.

"She's waiting, all set for your entrance, Mr. Trottingham," Brooks said.

Trottingham saw Levy's hand glide over Churchill's backside. For a moment he was mesmerized; the hand became his own. "Well," he said, "shall we go in?"

Outerbridge sat in the car. He laughed to himself. Still laughing he climbed out of the car and leaned against its top. He wondered if Summerall was already inside where he could see the fun.

Just opposite the entrance, fighting to keep the camera clear of people, Cromwell and the station manager were glaring at each other. The sound man, downing gin and tonics or anything else that was passed in his general direction, was screaming above the band and the voices, "Goddamn it, I'm hungry!"

"Shut up!" Cromwell shouted back.

"Uh—er—uhn," the station manger said.

"Shut up, you!" Cromwell said, fighting with her elbows to keep the space cleared.

"Damn it to hell! Damn it to hell!" the cameraman shouted. His eye was to the camera and he was focused on the entrance to the lawn, but people kept bumping him. He felt his eye starting to swell up. "Where is that asshole?"

"Stand clear, please! Stand clear!" Cromwell shouted, swinging roundhouses now, which tended to end somewhere near where a drink was being extended to her.

Bendersen screeched on, doing some reggae now in honor of Berhama, though Lapidus had told him that it would be considered revolutionary music and offensive to the kind of people who came to the party. But no one heard the words.

"Okay, Kirkland," Mandarino said, spotting the flailing Cromwell and her beleaguered crew. Mandarino gave him a slight push and he was onto the lawn, smiling slightly, hesitant.

"Come on, turkey," Cromwell screamed, waving. "Walk this way!"

Trottingham widened his smile and started toward her. From under one of the tables, he thought, something black and round looped up into the air behind him; then another.

"That's it, keep going right at the camera," he heard Mandarino say behind him.

It seemed that something suddenly cut a hole in the noise and there was a pocket of shocked silence behind him, then beside him and out further onto the lawn and up the lawn. His foot struck something heavy and Trottingham bent to pick it up as Corduro said,

"Look this way, Prime Minister, this way, this way—"

And Trottingham brought the grenade up and looked at it with disbelief in the same second the holes of silence filled again with sound.

"Hand grenades! Run! Duck! Make way! Fire in the hole!" and the blue blazers and white pants and white shoes and now visible white socks flashed everywhere.

"Keep shooting, keep shooting!" Cromwell screamed and grabbed the station manager to keep him between her and the grenade the Prime Minister was still holding.

Mandarino felt his guts turn to ice. Maybe he had had this nightmare: representative democracy, aided and abetted with a little public relations, being blown apart by people who no longer believed representative democracy worked. He clutched Suzanne and said in an embarrassingly choked voice, "Run, Sooz, run!"

Behind him, Brooks and Levy—Churchill between them—paused at the sudden change in the pitch of the voices around them, and stared at Mandarino as he flung Suzanne to the ground and shouted to them and, almost in the same breath, shouted at Trottingham, "Throw it, Trotts, throw it!"

"Mah drill hammah!" Bendersen shrieked. "Ah,'ll do it to ya, ah'll do it to ya!"

Even as he was forced back and down by the gyrating bodies around him, the photographer kept his finger on the release; the winder kept hissing.

The cameraman, shouting, "What the fuck's goin' on? What's goin' on?" kept his finger on the release until he saw the black oval object in the Prime Minister's hand, saw the look in his eyes, and then, still squeezing, backed forcefully into the crowd bowling over everyone behind him.

Trottingham in his fear found anger that someone would try to blow him up. "Bloody shits!" he roared and with an excess of motion flung the grenade from him, its flight creating a sudden opening in the crush of people before him. But they only bumped into each other and fell back down. They turned and looked at the grenade and waited, whimpering, for it to explode, and this scene was repeated up and down the lawn while Jax Bendersen sang about his drill hammer.

Up in the room, Rattery watched and waited for the sounds that would signal the end of the old Berhama and the start of the new.

Peter Frithe slipped from beneath a table and continued to pour and hand out drinks to those who were so drunk that they were oblivious to everything.

"The pin's not been pulled," someone shouted.

"The bloody fuckin' pin's not even in it," another cried.

Nervous laughter eased along the lawn.

Mandarino helped Suzanne to her feet. "What was it?" she said.

"A dummy hand grenade," Mandarino said. He did not laugh.

Brooks lifted his head out of a galvanized tub of ice cubes.

Levy and Churchill trembled in each other's arms.

The soundman picked up the grenade, shook it and watched the sand trickle out. "I'm hungry," he screamed, "and I am also drunk."

Cromwell, her knees feeling like jelly, held on to the station manager and smiled weakly. "Hi," she said. "That was some joke."

"Hey, you," Mandarino called to Corduro. "What'd you get?"

"How the hell should I know? You want the roll?

Here." He wound up and opened the camera and threw the roll to Mandarino. "I don't get paid for this shit," the photographer said. He shouldered his way through the crowd and vanished.

Mandarino walked toward Cromwell. It felt surprisingly good to be walking. The air was sweet. He looked with new interest into the faces around him. "What'd he get?" Mandarino gestured toward the cameraman.

"Hell, I don't know."

"Let's get the Prime Minister and get outa here. I got an idea. Can I get a playback on that machine?"

Cromwell turned to the station manager. "Can he?"

"Certainly." The station manager was already tabulating what he would bill network for this outing, and not only for the equipment and manpower.

They pushed out of the crush, through the hotel and into the parking lot where Outerbridge, holding his stomach, was still laughing.

"Hey babes," Mandarino said to Churchill, "get this developed at your office, will you? And bring it right back to the hotel."

"My room," Levy gasped.

"What was that all about?" Trottingham said.

244

Mandarino pushed him into the car. "Get in, Sooz. Hey Kevin, you go with her." He straightened and wheeled around to catch sight of Cromwell and her crew. He waved at them. "Come to the hotel. Let's have a look."

"He's hungry," Cromwell yelled."

"We'll feed him," Brooks said.

"Mike you go with them. Make sure they come right away. Hey you, driver, let's go." Mandarino scrambled into the car.

"What—?"

"It's all right, Kirkland," Mandarino said. "You all right, Sooz?"

"Yeah, wow."

While the soundman called room service and ordered two of everything plus a triple round of drinks, Mandarino and Cromwell and the camerman plugged in and played back the tape.

Trottingham said, "I don't understand. What's all this? What was going on at the party?"

Mandarino paused to look at him. "Kirkland, someone threw out some hand grenades. They were dummies. But nobody knew that right away. If they had been real, we wouldn't be here. Now, depending on what this camera shows—" he turned back when Cromwell pulled him away.

"There, there it is."

"Run it back," Mandarino said. "Kirkland, come here."

Trottingham moved forward, still puzzled, remembering that Mandarino had called him "Trotts" and Cromwell had called him a turkey.

"That's you."

Trottingham watched himself stare first in fear and then in anger at the object in his hand, and then fling it away.

"Good!" Mandarino cried as the images on the small screen became a jiggle and blur. He looked over at the cameraman. "Get a magnum of champagne buddy. Good job."

"Hold it, hold it," Cromwell said. "That is *my* tape. You get second use, Gary."

Mandarino grinned. "That's fine with me, babes. Run it first on network, then get me a print. Deal?"

"Deal."

The station manager cleared his throat.

Cromwell said to him, "Yeah, thanks. I owe you."

Mandarino led Trottingham out onto the balcony and closed the door. "Kirkland, that could have been for real, not a joke. Not a joke at all. You've got to get your people to stop thinking this is all a game. As it turns out, this may be very good for us. She'll run this on national television. It'll be run down here. What that segment shows is you being a hero. You didn't know that goddamn thing was a dud. You *acted* while the rest of us were running and hiding. The voters are gonna like that." Mandarino looked at him, wondering where within his being Trottingham had pulled the will to act as he had. "That was," he said, "a very good show."

"Well." Trottingham straightened. He smiled. Maybe Mandarino wasn't such a bad sort after all. He held out his hand. "Nice of you to say so, Gary."

"Maybe you'd better get on home and take a little rest before the mob shows up, Kirkland."

"Quite right. You'll all be coming, won't you? I mean, we have some rum now and—well, please come."

When Trottingham had gone, Mandarino went back inside and collected Suzanne and Brooks. They went to Brooks' room. "Let them eat," Mandarino said, falling down on the bed and closing his eyes.

"You all right, Gary?"

Mandarino opened his eyes and looked at Suzanne. He held out his hand. She took it. Brooks looked on. "I'm okay, Sooz. Inside, I'm shaking.

247

I was scared shitless. I can't tell you how scared I was."

"You were up front. You could see everything," Brooks said.

Mandarino raised himself. "So? Trottingham picked *up* one of those goddamn things. What'd he do? He got mad." He lay back down. "I got scared."

"I seem to remember you telling him to throw it," Suzanne said.

"And he did," Brooks said.

Mandarino smiled. "Can you imagine what it's gonna be like when we take on that Cuba account?"

"Har, har, har," Brooks said. "Yeah, I thought about it."

"Was that supposed to be a joke or a hint of things to come, Mike?"

"Me, I hope it was a joke." He turned at the knock on the door. "Kevin? That girl?"

Suzanne Kendrick looked at her watch. "Not yet."

"My friend," Brooks said, opening the door. "Hey, Fern."

Cromwell marched into the room and flopped down on the bed beside Mandarino. "I didn't think they'd be playing hardball down here."

"You were magnificent," Kendrick said.

"Maybe," Cromwell said, "but I am beat now."

"Where's your crew?"

"They're cleaning out your room, Gary: food, champagne and all." She held up a handful of tape cassette. "But I got the stuff, kiddo."

Mandarino said, "When're you going back to D.C.?"

"When are you going back to New York, lover?" she asked Brooks.

"Tomorrow. The early flight."

"Does that mean you'll be going back tomorrow, too, Fern?" Suzanne winked at her.

"Guess so." She sat up. "Isn't there a party around here somewhere? Where they won't be throwing hand grenades?"

"Trottingham's having a party. Why don't you go freshen up? We'll go when Kevin gets back with Churchill," Mandarino said.

"I'll help you," Brooks said, moving to the door.

"I think this time I can manage, Mike. See you in a while. Don't leave without me."

Brooks opened the door and stepped aside. "Okay?" he asked softly.

"Just aftershock. I'll be all right."

"You *were* fabulous, you know."

She patted his cheek. "I know."

Refreshed by his shower and clean clothes, Kirkland Trottingham sat on the edge of his dock. Behind him and up in the house, Greta Trottingham was superivisng the help as it prepared the final touches for the party.

Suppose it had been live, Trottingham kept asking himself. Then he would answer: but it wasn't. He looked across the bay at the island—his island. He fretted that someone disliked him intensely enough to have pretended to kill him. What had he done wrong? Was Mandarino right? How could he do better—and how quickly? Was there a better man than he to run Berhama at the moment? The future would take care of itself, but maybe the future depended on how well he did in the present. But the matter would have to be investigated, of course, then he would know more. Maybe.

Secretly, Trottingham had thought of himself as the Ian Smith of the Western Hemisphere, surrounded by clamoring Blacks and a few terrified whites. Maybe, like Smith, he'd been pushed too late into the world. Would Smith continue in his ways if the Blacks threw hand grenades at him? For Trottingham presumed that only the black Berhamians would have done such a thing.

It galled him to think that perhaps old Douglas

MacKenzie was right; that they could not keep all, indeed, most of what they had without speedily giving up a great deal more than they had even thought about. Even America had been close to that point not so long ago.

Trottingham stirred, watched the fish playing in a corner of the dock. He picked up the phone near where he sat and pressed the intercom for the garage.

"Outerbridge, I'd like you to go get Peter Frithe. Take him home to change and bring him back here for the party." He paused, feeling that he should give an explanation. "I don't think I want a member of my board of directors to be serving bar. Just tell him that, would you? Thanks."

Well, Trottingham thought. It was a start.

Peter Frithe and Graham Rattery looked at each other across the shambles of the tables Frithe served from. Word of the dummy grenades had passed up and down the lawn but few had left, and Jax Bendersen was now singing something about a diving firebird. Drunks, men and women, staggered up to the serving tables and then weaved away from them with fresh glasses.

They looked at each other and Rattery understood that he could not do it without them—and they didn't want to do it. Not his way. Yet, Rattery felt an undefined sense of relief floating over what he thought was his anger. He came close to Frithe, hesitated for a moment then said, "I don't understand."

Frithe said, "Who really does?" He studied the puzzled expression on Rattery's face. "Why didn't I tell you no? Because you might have found someone else who would've—like the kids. Hey, use the money for the farm. And let's stay friends." Frithe reached across the table and slid his hand into Rattery's.

"When Sinclair calls," Cynthia Archibald was telling her mother, "tell him that David and I have gone home." She carried the last suitcase out to the car and put it in the back seat. No. She was not going to the airport to catch Sandy taking the early rather than the late flight out. She was going to pick up a few groceries before the stores closed and have something ready for Sinclair to eat when he got home.

"I'll be happy to tell him," her mother said. "He may be working a little late tonight, though, like your father, because of the race and all the coming and going, you know."

"I think he'll manage to get home maybe even a little early tonight, Mother." She winked and kissed her. She started the car and backed out of the drive way and drove briskly into Wellington to

Luis DeSilva's *French Gourmet* market. As she shopped, pushing the baby around in the cart, she saw DeSilva nd Donnelly in a corner. They seemed despondent and she wondered why. Usually they were smart-assed, loudly cracking jokes and passing macho patter along to the women. Cynthia Archibald liked them the way they were, huddled in the corner; they seemed harmless, like two boys caught and chastened.

When they had arrived at the *Times* office, Linda Churchill was immediately pressed into service by her editor; word of the "Incident" with the grenades, as it was already being called, had preceded them.

"Why don't you go back to the hotel and tell them I won't have the photos for a while. I'll find you somewhere later."

"Jesus, Linda, don't forget the pictures, the pictures, okay?"

"Don't worry, Kevin. I'll bring prints."

They waited at the Queen for a while. Levy called, but the story Churchill was working on had been expanded to include the statement plus the afternoon's developments and a report from the CID. "But, I have what you want," she said. "Great photo."

It was close to seven when she arrived at Trottinghams. Among the well-tailored boat people she looked like a waif, with her drawn face and stringy hair and inked fingertips. She carried the envelope under her arm and passed from one crowded room to another until she found Levy, Brooks, Cromwell, Suzanne Kendrick and Mandarino.

Mandarino wanted to rush forward and seize the envelope. Instead he glanced at Levy.

"Linda, a drink?" Levy said.

"The biggest." She handed Levy the envelope and he handed it to Mandarino and went off to get her a drink.

Mandarino said to her, "Good, huh?"

"Yes. You'll want to pay Corduro for them."

"No problem." Mandarino moved to a light and opened the envelope and slipped out the photos. Even better than the tape, he thought. Yeah.

Beside him Brooks whispered, "That's gotta win it for him."

Trottingham had been caught with an angry glint in his eyes, his body in mid-shift so that his left arm pointed upward toward the camera, while his right, foreshortened, his white fingers tightly gripping the grenade, was angled almost behind him. The curls in his hair seemed filled with a motion of their own.

Mandarino leaned over to Churchill who'd found

a seat. "We'll buy the pictures. I don't even have to look at the rest. And we'll hire him."

"He may not want to work for you. He's pretty independent."

"Okay, okay. The pictures, I want. We'll work out the rest."

"Look, Mr. Mandarino, leave off, will you? We are impressed. You can't buy everyone or everything. Corduro was lucky and that's all." Churchill accepted the drink from Levy and did not look at anyone. Mandarino studied her. He felt Suzanne's arm slipping through his.

"You're right, Miss Churchill," he said, sighing. "Absolutely right. Sorry." He looked around. "It's been a long day. Longer than I wanted it to be." He put his arm around Suzanne. "We're going. Let's make the eleven o'clock plane out, what do you say?"

Levy nodded.

"Perfect," Brooks said.

Mandarino glanced around for Trottingham. "See you in the morning then."

As they walked to the car, Suzanne Kendrick said lightly, "Your place or mine?"

"Which do you want?"

"Both, but I'll take yours. Let's go."

They sat holding hands in the darkness of the balcony. Dance music, wafted by the wind through the hotel, came to them. They heard the rubbery creep of traffic through the streets and watched the figures, tiny with distance, move up and down the steps leading to the Royal Berhama Yacht Club.

In every campaign, Mandarino was thinking, there comes that moment. The opponent breaks down and cries on national television; the opponent is linked with the "baddies" or decides to take a midnight swim in the Lincoln Memorial pool.

Or our guys come up with a cut in taxes or a tax rebate, or are seen with just the right kind of person, man or woman, or he's a lousy baseball player, but it's the American game and so, bingo, points. The campaign here, even though it had not even been officially kicked off, had been won already, Mandarino knew; it was won on the lawn of the Royal Berhamian Hotel this afternoon. By the time he got through, half a generation of Berhamians would know and come to remember Kirkland Trottingham. Corduro's picture would overwhelm them in posters, magazines, papers, not only here, but around the world.

It didn't matter that the grenades were all duds; that was found life. The picture was taken on the edge of oblivion—a point they would make again and again. And they would imply that the grenades

256

had been a joke as much as a threat of things to come. He must make that point to Trottingham and his people, Mandarino thought. Then maybe they would start treating all the black Berhamians just the way they had treated Frithe at Trottingham's party.

By tomorrow night it would be public knowledge that Mandarino Associates were working for the Berhama United Party. There might be an uproar, but better then than the day before the election. But the Frithe announcement and the Abu Dabi deal—whatever it would be would not be bad—put the frosting on the cake. They would go through the motions, yes. But the whole damned thing was in the bag.

Mandarino knew, however, that he would never take on another campaign without thinking of the extent to which political hatreds could run. Well, much of that had begun back home, at least in recent times, with the Kennedys and King and Malcolm X. Possibly Hale Boggs and Walter Reuther, too. Who in the hell knew?

He needed some stability in his personal life, something, like love, to help balance what he saw as the coming terror. He felt Suzanne's hands stroking his back, heard drunken laughter from the street, and the music. "Let's do it," he said. "Be together."

"That would be nice," Suzanne Kendrick said.

257

And it would be. But she didn't want him to feel that he owed her anything because she was mutilated and he was sorry for her. Rafe had left with both her blessings and curses, but he had been up front about it; he said he simply didn't know how he could handle it. How long would it take before Gary could handle it, if ever? And if he never said that he couldn't, would she be able to tell and so release him? Perhaps they would be spared that if the little nasties came again and this time claimed the whole rather than just parts. Yes, maybe that was the event to wait for. She said, "Think about it, babes. Until I get back. And I will, too, and then we'll see."

"I know what you're thinking," Mandarino said.

"Maybe, maybe not, but let's go to bed. Let's leave the door to the balcony open so we can see the moonlight and hear all the parties and smell the ocean."

In the morning, Brooks and Levy gathered in Mandarino's room for breakfast. Suzanne Kendrick had driven home. Linda Churchill had gone to her office, and Fern Cromwell was meeting a final time with the station manager.

"I guess you'll be back next week, huh, Kevin?"

"Well, you want the Frithe thing done right. I guess so."

Mandarino and Brooks exchanged glances. "I know you'll do a dyn-o-mite job," Brooks said.

Mandarino closed the paper he'd skimmed through. "They say they don't have a clue as to who was responsible for that business yesterday. Ah, well. We all packed? Let's finish the coffee and get moving."

"What's with you and Sooz?" Levy asked.

"Well, we'll have to see, Kevin. She's had a double mastectomy. Doesn't want pity."

"Aw, shit," Brooks said.

"I was never a big tit man," Mandarino said. "Was I? I don't remember."

"I dunno," Levy said. "That's tough, Gary. But she's coming back, right?"

"Yeah. I guess we'll work things out." He stood and looked around the room. "I guess we can hit the road, you guys."

Outside it was already hot and the sun was bright, its rays beating down on Berhama. The cab they were in moved slowly down Dock Street, through the steady flow of tourists laden with cameras and plastic shopping bags. Taxis lined up near the dock where the *Rotterdam* and the *Statendam* and the *QE II* were tied up. The drivers of the horse-drawn carriages, their hats or caps pulled down to shade their eyes from the sun, sat motionlessly in

259

their seats under the poinsettia trees. They drove past the banks, the rows of stores, the moped rental establishments and, gradually, they were out of Wellington and into the countryside where the pastel-colored houses sat along the road and upon the hillsides.

The cab driver said, "Did you enjoy your visit to Berhama?"

"Yes," Levy said, briefly. They all lapsed into silence again.

The driver began to hum, then he said, "People always come back to Berhama. It's a nice, quiet place where nothing ever happens, and that's why people like it so much."

Mandarino grunted, closed his eyes and wondered what Suzanne Kendrick was doing at that very moment.